COMANCHE MOON

COMANCHE MOON

A Picture Narrative About

⊱ CYNTHIA ANN PARKER ⊰

Her Twenty-five Year Captivity Among
the Comanche Indians ~ and her son,

⊱ QUANAH PARKER ⊰

The Last Chief of the Comanches

—◆—

WRITTEN AND ILLUSTRATED
by
JACK JACKSON

—◆—

INTRODUCTION
by
T. R. Fehrenbach

Reed

Graphica

Edited by Calvin Reid
Composition by John Reinhardt Book Design

A Reed Graphica Book
Published by Reed Press™
360 Park Avenue South
New York, NY 10010

www.reedpress.com

ISBN: 1-59429-003-2

Portions of "Comanche Moon" originally appeared as "White Comanche," "Red Raider," and "Blood on the Moon," a comic book trilogy published by Last Gasp, San Francisco, CA.

Printed in the United States of America

10 9 8 7 6 5 4 3 2 1

970.3   History N. Am/
Specific Native peoples

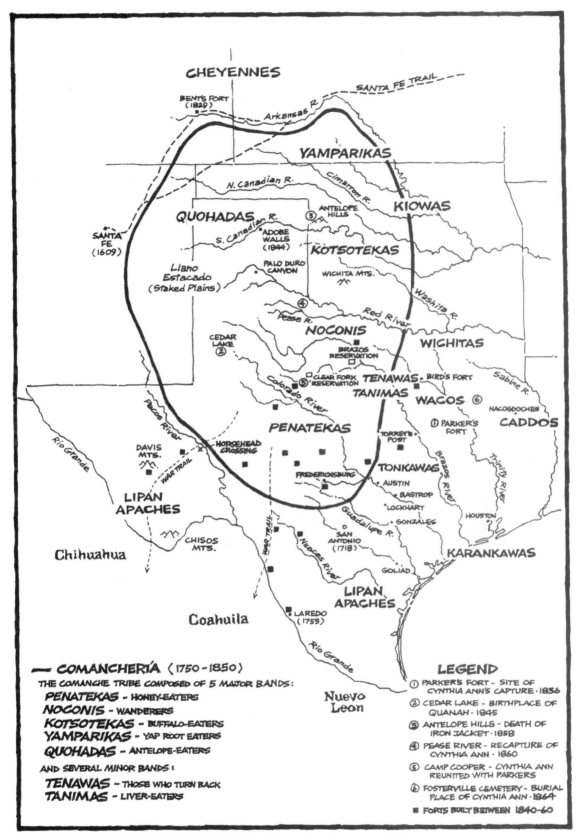

CHEYENNES

BENT'S FORT (1829)

SANTA FE TRAIL

Arkansas R.

YAMPARIKAS

N. Canadian R.

Cimarron R.

KIOWAS

QUOHADAS

ANTELOPE HILLS
③

S. Canadian R.

ADOBE WALLS (1844)

KOTSOTEKAS

SANTA FE (1609)

Llano Estacado (Staked Plains)

PALO DURO CANYON

WICHITA MTS.

Washita R.

④

Pease R.

Red River

NOCONIS

WICHITAS

CEDAR LAKE ②

BRAZOS RESERVATION

Colorado River

⑤ CLEAR FORK RESERVATION

TENAWAS

BIRD'S FORT

Sabine R.

TANIMAS

WACOS ⑥

NACOGDOCHES

Pecos River

DAVIS MTS.

WAR TRAIL

HORSEHEAD CROSSING

PENATEKAS

TORREY'S POST

① PARKER'S FORT

CADDOS

FREDERICKSBURG

TONKAWAS

AUSTIN

BASTROP

Brazos River

Trinity River

LIPAN APACHES

CHISOS MTS.

Chihuahua

WAR TRAIL

Nueces River

SAN ANTONIO (1718)

LOCKHART

GONZALES

Guadalupe R.

HOUSTON

GOLIAD

KARANKAWAS

LIPAN APACHES

Coahuila

LAREDO (1759)

Rio Grande

Nuevo Leon

— COMANCHERÍA (1750-1850)

THE COMANCHE TRIBE COMPOSED OF 5 MAJOR BANDS:

PENATEKAS - HONEY-EATERS
NOCONIS - WANDERERS
KOTSOTEKAS - BUFFALO-EATERS
YAMPARIKAS - YAP ROOT EATERS
QUOHADAS - ANTELOPE-EATERS

AND SEVERAL MINOR BANDS:

TENAWAS - THOSE WHO TURN BACK
TANIMAS - LIVER-EATERS

LEGEND

① PARKER'S FORT - SITE OF CYNTHIA ANN'S CAPTURE · 1836
② CEDAR LAKE - BIRTHPLACE OF QUANAH · 1845
③ ANTELOPE HILLS - DEATH OF IRON JACKET · 1858
④ PEASE RIVER - RECAPTURE OF CYNTHIA ANN · 1860
⑤ CAMP COOPER - CYNTHIA ANN REUNITED WITH PARKERS
⑥ FOSTERVILLE CEMETERY - BURIAL PLACE OF CYNTHIA ANN · 1864
■ FORTS BUILT BETWEEN 1840-60

THE COMANCHE RANGE AS IT EXTENDED FOR OVER A CENTURY. THE EASTERN BOUNDARY LINE WAS GRADUALLY ERODED BY WHITE PENETRATIONS, BUT REMAINED A WAR ZONE UNTIL THE FINAL CAMPAIGNS OF 1874-75. THE TWO TEXAS RESERVATIONS WERE CLOSED IN 1858.

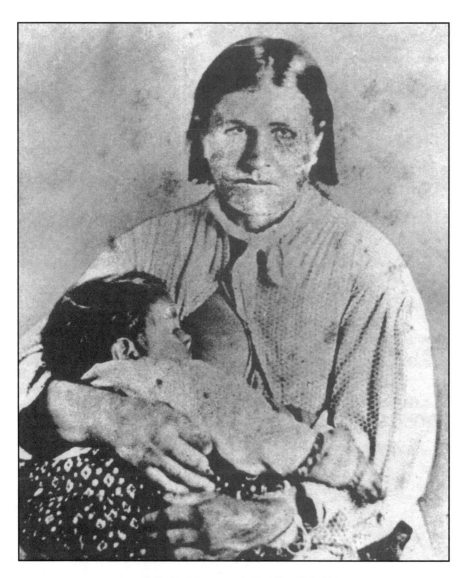

CYNTHIA ANN PARKER

This daguerreotype of Cynthia Ann and her daughter Topsannah was made by A. F. Corning of Ft. Worth in 1862. It was this picture that Capt. Sul Ross lated secured a copy of and sent to Quanah in response to his newspaper inquiry. A rancher friend had it duplicated in oils for Quanah who displayed it with great pride to visitors in his home. (UTA)

The wars between the Comanches and Anglo-Americans were the bloodiest and most protracted of any between invading Europeans and American aborigines on this continent.

They marked the culmination of three hundred years of bloodshed between white men and red; they were not the high noon, but the twilight of the plains tribes.

The final chapter of this long warfare began in Texas, when thousands of farming families entered upon the Comanche range. Here two peoples met, and each to itself was true. The ways of the Comanches spawned horror and dark racial hatreds among the whites: the relentless advance of civilization spelled doom for the Indians and their mode of life.

Through this entire warfare the family tragedy of the Parker clan runs like a dark thread. The raid on Parker's Fort in 1836, and the carrying off of little Cynthia Ann sounded a tocsin from which the frontier flamed. That flame was only extinguished with the surrender of Quanah Parker, the last warchief of the Comanches, on the graveyard plains.

In one sense, all this warfare was only a footnote in the building of a vast industrial nation-state.

In another, it was war as primordial, deadly, and decisive as any in history, in which the fate of a vast Southwestern empire was decreed.

Above all, it was a tragedy: not a struggle between right and wrong, but between two rights upon the North American continent and of two sturdy, valiant, warlike peoples to survive, and to live in the ways they believed ordained.

Thus it is a story that will never die, and it will be retold as long as men are men.

T. R. Fehrenbach
(A historian specializing in the Texas republic and Military history)

COMANCHE MOON

THE TRUE STORY OF CYNTHIA ANN PARKER, HER
SON QUANAH, AND THE WILD COMANCHES OF TEXAS!

WRITTEN AND ILLUSTRATED by JACK JACKSON

THE CAPTURE OF HIS MOTHER

CYNTHIA ANN

Spring, 1836: TEXAS IS IN TURMOIL. THE BATTLE OF SAN JACINTO HAS JUST BEEN WON, AND THE SETTLERS THAT HAD FLED AT THE APPROACH OF SANTA ANNA'S ARMY HAVE RETURNED TO THEIR HOMES ON THE FRONTIER ~ HOMES LIKE THIS ONE AT PARKER'S FORT.

BUT ANOTHER MENACE AWAITS THEM, A FAR MORE DEADLY FOE THAN THE SHATTERED LEGIONS OF MEXICO ~ THE DREADED COMANCHES, War Lords of the Southern Plains!

THE TRIBES HAVE LEARNED OF THE CHAOS IN THE WAKE OF THE *Texas Revolution*, AND WASTE NO TIME SENDING FIERCE RAIDING PARTIES OUT TO PROBE WEAKNESSES IN THE EXPOSED SETTLEMENTS.

THEY WANT DIRECTIONS AND A BEEVE TO EAT... I THINK THEY'RE UP TO NO GOOD, BUT MAYBE I CAN TALK THEM OUT OF IT..

BEN, DON'T GO BACK OUT THERE

11

THE HORROR-STRUCK PARKER CLAN SEES THEIR WORST FEARS MATERIALIZE RIGHT BEFORE THEIR EYES...

OH MY GOD, THEY'VE KILLED HIM...GATHER UP THE CHILDREN, QUICK!

IN THE CONFUSION THAT FOLLOWS THE BRUTAL SLAYING OF ELDER PARKER'S SON, NO ONE THINKS TO CLOSE THE STOCKADE GATE.

ONCE INSIDE THE COMPOUND, THE RAIDERS ~ THEIR BLOODLUST FIRED BY EASY SUCCESS ~ MAKE SHORT WORK OF THE FEEBLE RESISTANCE.

LUCY PARKER ATTEMPTS TO ESCAPE THROUGH THE REAR GATE WITH HER FOUR YOUNG CHILDREN.

CYNTHIA!! HURRY CHILDREN, RUN!

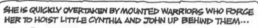

SHE IS QUICKLY OVERTAKEN BY MOUNTED WARRIORS WHO FORCE HER TO HOIST LITTLE CYNTHIA AND JOHN UP BEHIND THEM...

MOMMA, MOMMA!

PLEASE, DON'T TAKE MY BABIES...

ONLY THE TIMELY ARRIVAL OF DAVID FAULKENBERRY SAVES LUCY PARKER AND HER OTHER TWO CHILDREN.

GIT! GIT AWAY!!

MEANWHILE, THE FORT IS LOOTED FOR WEAPONS, POWDER, LEAD, SCRAP IRON, SWEETS AND GEE-GAWS..THE REST, DESTROYED.

GATHERING UP THEIR BOOTY AND TERRIFIED CAPTIVES, THE BOLD WARRIORS DASH AWAY BEFORE THE ALARM CAN BE SPREAD TO THE MENFOLK IN THE FIELDS.

AND IN THEIR WAKE, THERE IS ONLY DESOLATION, DEATH, AND DESTRUCTION.

GOD.. HELP THEM.. GASP!.. IN THE BOSOM OF TH' COMANCHE..

ONCE THEY HAVE RIDDEN FAR ENOUGH TO FEEL SAFE FROM RETALIATION, THE RAIDERS CELEBRATE THEIR VICTORY WITH A SCALPDANCE BENEATH THE STARS.

WHAT ARE THEY DOING, RACHEL?

THE CHILDREN ARE FORCED TO WATCH THE HUMILIATION OF ELIZABETH KELLOGG AND RACHEL PLUMMER, TIME AND TIME AGAIN.

OH MY GOD.. PLEASE..NO! NO..OOHH..

AT THE FIRST LIGHT, THE WARRIORS BREAK CAMP, DIVIDE THE SPOILS, AND HEAD THEIR SEPARATE WAYS. CYNTHIA IS CLAIMED BY A BAND OF PENATAKAS, BOUND FOR WEST TEXAS.

...FOUR GUNS AND THE LITTLE SQUAW..

OKAY, BUT THIS ONE COMES WITH US!!

POWDER

LITTLE JOHN IS TAKEN BY ANOTHER BAND, AND HER LAST TIE WITH THE WHITE WORLD IS SEVERED AS HE IS CARRIED AWAY.

CYNTHIA ANN FIGHTS OFF HER TEARS AND TRIES TO BE BRAVE AS HER CAPTORS RIDE DEEPER INTO STRANGE SURROUNDINGS.

MAMMA ALWAYS SAID CRYING DOESN'T HELP.. ..SNIFF..

14

AFTER SEVERAL DAYS OF HARD TRAVELING, THEY COME TO A VILLAGE.

VICTORY, MY BROTHERS AND MANY COUPS!

CYNTHIA IS BANDIED ABOUT AND HANDLED ROUGHLY BUT GOOD HUMOREDLY BY THE VILLAGERS, TO WHOM THE SIGHT OF A WHITE PERSON IS STILL A NOVELTY.

THE RIGORS OF NOMADIC LIFE TAKE A HEAVY TOLL ON THE COMANCHE BIRTHRATE, AND CAPTIVE CHILDREN ARE ALWAYS WELCOMED TO REPLENISH THE TRIBES' SMALL NUMBERS.

A STURDY CHILD, ASA.

SHE WILL BEAR US MANY WARRIORS!

ONE MIDDLE-AGED WARRIOR, WHO HAS JUST LOST A YOUNG DAUGHTER, SEES HER AS THE ANSWER TO HIS WIFE'S PRAYERS.

MAYBE SHE WOULD TAKE THE WOMAN'S MIND OFF NADUAH..

AT LENGTH, SERIOUS BARGAINING BEGINS, AND HE STRIKES A PRICE WITH THE RAID'S LEADER. CYNTHIA HAS A NEW HOME.

HOW ABOUT IF I THROW IN TWO AXES?

DONE!

NADUAH, WHITE COMANCHE

> YOU... NADUAH!

AND SO BEGINS CYNTHIA ANN PARKER'S NEW LIFE AS A WHITE COMANCHE. HER ADOPTED PARENTS, TABBY-NOCCA AND CHATUA, ARE NOT CRUEL TO HER, AS IS THE CASE WITH MANY OLDER CAPTIVES. THEY GIVE HER THE NAME OF THE LOST DAUGHTER WHOSE PLACE SHE IS TO TAKE.

NADUAH, A RESOURCEFUL CHILD, RAPIDLY MAKES THE TRANSITION TO HER NEW CULTURE. FIRST COMES HER LANGUAGE LESSONS.

> KOO-OH-NY, KOO-OH-NY!

> KOO-OH-NY.. STICK!!

(PRONOUNCED, NAH-DU-WAH')

SHE IS GIVEN YOUNGSTER'S CHORES, LIKE GATHERING FIREWOOD.

> COME ON NADUAH, IT'S STARTING TO RAIN!

> KOO-OH-NY KOO-OH-NY..

SHE LEARNS TO HELP HER NEW MOTHER WITH THE MANY CAMP TASKS OF A PEOPLE ALWAYS ON THE GO.

AND LATER, TO FOLLOW IN THE WAKE OF THE CHASE WITH THE WOMEN AND SKIN THE FALLEN BUFFALO, STAFF OF LIFE TO THE WILD COMANCHE.

NOW, YOU CUT ALONG THE RIBS, AND THERE'S THE STOMACH, SEE?

AND TO SLICE THE MEAT THIN FOR DRYING.

NO SATA, YOU'VE ALREADY HAD ENOUGH..

WHINE.. DROOL...

SHE LEARNS TO PREPARE SKINS USED FOR CLOTHING AND GEAR.

..TO DECORATE THE GARMENTS WITH BEADWORK AND PAINTING.

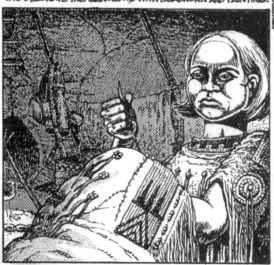

WHEN THE WORK IS DONE, TO BUNDLE UP AROUND WINTER CAMP-FIRES AND LISTEN TO THE ELDERS SPEAK OF THE MYSTERIOUS LAND AND THE COMANCHES' PLACE IN THE CREATOR'S DREAM.

SO THEN THE CLEVER COYOTE SEZ TO THE TURKEY, "BET YOU CAN'T LIFT YOUR LEG THIS HIGH..."

THE COMANCHES ARE A FUN-LOVING PEOPLE AND MUCH OF THEIR TIME IS SPENT AT FAVORITE RESORT AREAS. THEY ARE FOND OF CONSTANTLY MOVING ABOUT AND VISITING THEIR FRIENDS AND RELATIVES IN OTHER BANDS.

WELL, WELL, LOOK WHO'S HERE!!

SO THIS IS THAT NEW PAPOOSE I'VE BEEN HEARING ABOUT! MY, MY!

THOUGHT WE'D COME DOWN AND HELP YOU ALL EAT THE PECAN CROP THIS YEAR. HEH HEH

THEY RULE THE PLAINS AND HILL COUNTRY, BUT NO ONE RULES THE UNPREDICTABLE TEXAS WEATHER.

THE HORSES!! QUINNE, GET THE HORSES!!

ITS VIOLENT EXTREMES OF SCORCHING HEAT AND FREEZING NORTHERS SHAPE THE REDMAN JUST AS THEY SHAPE THE VAST LAND — INDOMITABLE, YET EVER CHANGING.

SLOWLY BUT SURELY THESE SAME FORCES MOLD YOUNG NADUAH AND SHE COMES TO LOVE THE LAND WITH THE SAME PASSION AS HER ADOPTED PEOPLE.

SHE LEARNS TO APPRECIATE THE BEAUTY OF THE RUGGED PLAINS, WITH THEIR MAJESTIC SUNSETS AND BLANKETS OF WILDFLOWERS.

WITH THE PASSING YEARS, NADUAH BLOOMS AND RIPENS INTO A YOUNG MAIDEN, VERSED IN ALL THE SKILLS OF COMANCHE WOMANHOOD.

LOOK PAPA, NADUAH FOUND YOU SOME RIPE PLUMS!

SHE'S GONNA MAKE SOME LUCKY WARRIOR A GOOD WIFE — AND HER DEAR OLD DADDY A MAN RICH IN HORSES.

HER MEMORIES OF THE 'LOST FAMILY' AND HER CHILDHOOD AT PARKER'S FORT FADE TO A MERE GLIMMER AS TIME SLIPS AWAY.

SHE'S GOT YOU, SUNA! HAHA!

OH NO! NOT AGAIN!

EXCEPT FOR HER PALE SKIN, BLUE EYES, AND BLONDE, GREASE-SMEARED HAIR, SHE IS NOTHING BUT PURE COMANCHE!!

THEN ONE DAY, A BAND OF FAR-RANGING QUOHADAS, RETURNING FROM A RAID DEEP INTO MEXICO, STOP AND VISIT THEIR PENATEKA COUSINS.

✴ THE GIRLS ARE PLAYING THE 'AWL GAME' IN WHICH PIECES ARE MOVED OVER AN OBSTACLE COURSE BY THE THROW OF MARKED STICKS.

THE YOUNG CHIEF OF THE QUOHADA BAND IS PETA NOCONA, AND SO DEVOTED ARE HIS FOLLOWERS THAT THEY CALL THEMSELVES *NOCONIS*, IN HONOR OF THEIR FEARLESS LEADER.

PETA NOCONA IS SMOTE WITH THE BEAUTY OF THE BLUE-EYED MAIDEN NADUAH, AND DETERMINES TO MAKE HER HIS WIFE.

NOW THERE'S A CUTE ONE..

HMM....NOT BAD FOR A WHITE GIRL...

I'LL HAVE TO CHECK INTO THIS..

ACCORDINGLY, HE BEGINS TO COURT HER, COMANCHE FASHION, PLAYING LOVE SONGS ON HIS FLUTE IN THE EARLY EVENINGS NEAR HER FATHER'S TEPEE..

IT IS A RICH BRIDAL PRICE, FROM A WARRIOR TOO ESTEEMED TO BE REBUFFED. NADUAH'S PARENTS SIGNIFY THEIR ACCEPTANCE OF THE MARRIAGE BY DRIVING PETA'S HORSES IN WITH THEIR OWN.

A GIRL COULD DO WORSE, THAT'S FOR SURE!

NADUAH LOOK! TEN HORSES AND ALL THOSE NICE BLANKETS!

I THOUGHT HE'D NEVER ASK..

TEN AIN'T BAD, BUT WE MIGHT COULD TRY HOLDING OUT FOR ELEVEN...

BEFORE LONG, NADUAH AWAKENS TO FIND A GIFT OF HORSES, LOADED WITH BLANKETS AND MEXICAN PLUNDER, STAKED OUTSIDE HER DOOR.

THUS, NADUAH BECOMES THE WIFE OF PETA NOCONA — AND THE ENVY OF ALL THE OTHER MARRIAGEABLE COMANCHE GIRLS, FOR HE IS REGARDED AS QUITE A CATCH.

HER LIFE WITH HIM IS HAPPY FROM THE START.

THERE'S ANOTHER ONE THAT GOT AWAY GIRLS...SIGH

HELLO, MY NAME'S PETA.

YES, I KNOW..

NADUAH, WIVES ARE NOT SUPPOSED TO BEAT THEIR HUSBANDS IN HORSERACES..

HA!

A FEW MONTHS AFTER THEIR MARRIAGE, THE MONOTONY OF CAMP LIFE IS BROKEN BY THE APPEARANCE OF WHITE TRADERS, A RARE EVENT FOR TIMES WHEN COMANCHES RULE THE PLAINS.

DON'T MAKE ANY SUDDEN MOVES, MEN..

I HOPE YOU KNOW WHAT WE'RE DOIN' SIR...

HI-YIII YIP, YIP
YAH-OOOU
EEEE-AH WOOP
HA-YA

CHIEF PAHA-YUCA, WHO HAS HAD CONSIDERABLE EXPERIENCE DEALING WITH WHITES, GREETS THE TRADERS AMICABLY.

DURING THE VISIT, COL. WILLIAMS, A FRIEND OF THE PARKER FAMILY, RECOGNIZES CYNTHIA AND TRIES TO RANSOM HER.

HOW, CHIEF...

WELCOME, BROTHERS. YOU GOT CANDY?

I'LL GIVE YOU TWELVE MULES AND TWO LOADS OF MERCHANDISE FOR HER.

DON'T GET YOUR HOPES UP, BUT I'LL SPEAK TO HER FOLKS.

WHAT DO THEY WANT, PETA?

DON'T WORRY, I'LL TAKE CARE OF IT..

?

PETA NOCONA REACTS WITH PREDICTABLE ANGER.

YOU TELL THEM THEY BETTER LEAVE, IF THEY WANT TO KEEP THEIR HAIR!

THAT'S WHAT I FIGURED YOU'D SAY...

SORRY.. NO DEAL. HER FAMILY IS VERY ATTACHED TO HER.

WELL, AT LEAST LET US SPEAK TO HER.

NADUAH IS UPSET AND DISTRESSED BY THESE STRANGE MEN WHO TALK OF TAKING HER AWAY FROM HER LOVED ONES.

REMEMBER YOUR MOTHER? DON'T YOU MISS HER? AND YOUR BROTHERS? WE WANT TO TAKE YOU BACK HOME TO THEM. THEY STILL LOVE YOU, CYNTHIA ANN..

I DON'T KNOW WHAT HE'S TALKING ABOUT, BUT I DON'T LIKE THE SOUND OF IT..

SHE CRIES AND RUNS AWAY TO HIDE.

NOW THAT'S STRANGE.. WONDER WHAT'S THE MATTER WITH HER?

THEY PROBABLY THREATENED HER IF SHE TALKED TO US.

MY FRIENDS, YOU GO NOW! THE YOUNG MEN ASK FOR YOUR SCALPS!

COL. WILLIAMS AND HIS MEN DEPART, NEVER GUESSING THAT THE REASON FOR NADUAH'S BEHAVIOR IS HER KNOWLEDGE THAT SHE IS WITH CHILD — THE CHILD THAT WILL LATER BE KNOWN AS QUANAH.

CAN'T FIGURE IT OUT.. THE KIDS ALWAYS WANT TO STAY WITH THEM.

ONE OF THESE DAYS WE OUGHTA TEACH THEM DAMN SAVAGES SOME MANNERS, COL.

PAHA-YUGA BREAKS CAMP AND HEADS WEST, AWAY FROM THE PRYING TEXANS.

THEY MIGHT COME BACK WITH SOLDIERS TO TAKE NADUAH AWAY..

LET'S GO TO THE LAND OF MY PEOPLE, THE QUOHADAS. THERE WE WILL BE SAFE, PAHA-YUCA.

NEAR CEDAR LAKE IN FAR WEST TEXAS, THE TIME GROWS NEAR FOR ~

A SON NAMED QUANAH

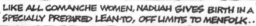

LIKE ALL COMANCHE WOMEN, NADUAH GIVES BIRTH IN A SPECIALLY PREPARED LEAN-TO, OFF LIMITS TO MENFOLK..

AND PRESENTS HER PROUD HUSBAND WITH A SON, NAMED FOR THE FRAGRANCE OF THE PLAINS WILDFLOWERS, WHICH SHE LOVES SO MUCH.

LET'S CALL HIM QUANAH..

IT'S GOOD, WIFE.. YOU DO REAL GOOD.

23

THEN SHE IS SOUGHT OUT BY HER BROTHER JOHN, WHO HAD BEEN RANSOMED BACK AFTER SIX YEARS WITH THE INDIANS, BUT NEVER FULLY READJUSTED TO TAME, WHITE SOCIETY.

JOHN FINDS HIS SISTER INDIFFERENT TO NOTIONS OF EVER ABANDONING HER LIFE AS A COMANCHE 'SQUAW!'

YEAH, THEY MADE ME CUT MY HAIR...I'M ASHAMED TO BE SEEN, LOOKING LIKE A SQUAW, BUT THEY INSISTED THAT I COME FIND YOU..

WELCOME BACK LITTLE BROTHER— HAIR OR NO HAIR.

HA HA

THIS IS WHERE I BELONG. HERE I GOT FRIENDS THAT LOVE ME, A BEAUTIFUL BABY BOY, A GREAT OLDMAN— EVEN IF HE DOES BEAT ON ME ONCE IN AWHILE...

I'D BE CRAZY TO LEAVE ALL THIS BEHIND!

MMM..YOU GOT A POINT THERE. THINK I'LL STAY AWHILE MYSELF!

OVER THE YEARS, WORD OF THE WHITE WOMAN, WIFE TO A GREAT CHIEF, CONTINUES TO FILTER OUT OF COMANCHERÍA. AGENT NEIGHBORS MENTIONS 'MISS PARKER' IN A REPORT AS STRANGELY SATISFIED WITH HER SITUATION, AND HAVING FAILED TO COAX HER AWAY, ADDS THAT IT WOULD REQUIRE FORCE TO SEPARATE HER FROM THE INDIANS.

A MORE CAPABLE MAN COULD NOT BE FOUND TO HANDLE THE INDIAN AFFAIRS OF TEXAS THAN MAJOR ROBERT NEIGHBORS, A SOLDIER OF THE REPUBLIC, A RANGER UNDER JACK HAYS, IN WHOSE COMPANY HE HAD BEEN CAPTURED WHILE DEFENDING SAN ANTONIO AGAINST THE WOLL INVASION. AFTER 18 MONTHS IN A MEXICAN PRISON, NEIGHBORS HAS ONLY RECENTLY RETURNED HOME, BUT ALREADY HE IS IN THE SERVICE OF TEXAS.

TIRELESSLY HE RIDES THE LONG FRONTIER, HIS PRESENCE A HOPEFUL SIGN TO THE INDIANS, NOW BECOMING ANXIOUS ABOUT THE FUTURE.

I AM BEAR'S HEAD, THE DELAWARE WHO SPEAKS MANY TONGUES, AND THIS IS NEIGHBORS, THE MIGHTY TEXAN WARRIOR WHO COMES TO THE COMANCHE AS A FRIEND!!

HOWDY, NEIGHBORS!

THEY'RE SURE HEALTHY-LOOKING FELLOWS...

ALMOST SINGLE-HANDEDLY, THROUGH SHEER STRENGTH OF PERSONALITY, HE WORKS TO KEEP THE FRAGILE PEACE.

HE SAYS THAT THE PRISONERS HITCHED UP TO THE CART PRETENDED TO BE SCARED BY THIS UGLY OLD HAG AND GALLOPED OFF! THEIR SIMPLE-MINDED GUARD WAS COMPLETELY FOOLED, AND TOLD HIS JEFE THAT THESE TEXANS WEREN'T SUCH FEARLESS DEVILS AFTER ALL!

HAHAHA HOHO GASP CACKLE

THAT'S GREAT! SOUNDS JUST LIKE THOSE GULLIBLE MEXICANS!

HAW HAW HAW

YUCK YUCK

SLAP

NOT ONLY IS HE EMINENTLY QUALIFIED AND WELL ACQUAINTED WITH THE SITUATION, BUT HE IS ALSO ONE OF THE FEW WHITEMEN IN TEXAS ACTUALLY CONCERNED ABOUT THE INDIANS' WELFARE.

TELL YOUR CHIEF THERE MUST BE A LINE. ON ONE SIDE, YOUR LAND, ON THE OTHER, OURS! OVER THIS LINE, NO WHITES MUST PASS... NOW, WHATEVER THE WHITEMAN SEES, HE TAKES — AND WHAT HE TAKES, HE WILL NOT SHARE!

THE WHITE-EYES PLACE THEIR LODGES ALONG THE STREAMS WHERE GAME IS PLENTIFUL AND THE GRASS IS RICH...

...THESE WERE THE CAMPING PLACES OF OUR FATHERS, BUT IF WE GO THERE NOW, THE WHITES SHOOT AT US! THIS — CANNOT BE!!

NEIGHBORS KNEW THAT IN THE DAYS WHEN SPAIN RULED TEXAS, THE COMANCHES WERE THE REAL MASTERS, AND WITH THE DESTRUCTION OF SAN SABA, THEY HAD VIRTUALLY STOPPED SPANISH EXPANSION NORTH OF BEXAR.

BEFORE THE TURN OF THE CENTURY, COMANCHES WERE SO BOLD THAT THEY WOULD PARADE IN THE STREETS OF THE CITY, OPENLY TAKING THEIR FILL OF TRIBUTE BEFORE THE VERY EYES OF THE HAPLESS CITIZENS.

BUT THE COMANCHES WERE RUDELY AWAKENED WHEN THEY TRIED THE SAME TACTICS ON THE NEW CONQUERORS OF TEXAS— THE ANGLOS, STILL FEISTY AFTER TWO HUNDRED YEARS OF INDIAN SUBJUGATION AND EXTERMINATION.

NEIGHBORS ALSO KNEW THAT THE COUNCIL HOUSE FIGHT—SOME SAID 'MASSACRE'—AT BEXAR IN 1840 HAD DESTROYED ANY COMANCHE ILLUSIONS OF PEACEFUL COEXISTENCE WITH THE WHITES. 33 DIED IN THE MELEE, 12 OF THEM NOTED PENATEKA CHIEFS.

HE UNDERSTOOD THAT THE *BIG RAID*, PLUNDERING ALL THE WAY TO THE GULF, HAD BEEN IN RETALIATION FOR THE TREACHERY AT COUNCIL HOUSE; AND THAT EVEN THOUGH THE RAIDERS HAD BEEN DRIVEN OFF, THEY HAD NOT BEEN SOUNDLY BEATEN.

IN THE FOLLOWING YEARS IT HAD BEEN AN UNEASY STANDOFF. THEN THE RANGERS GOT THE PATERSON COLT, A WEAPON THAT GAVE THE WHITES A 'SHOT FOR EACH FINGER'— AND SUPERIORITY OVER THE REDMEN IN CLOSE, RUNNING FIGHTS.

AND SO IT HAD GONE, UP TO THE PRESENT, WHEN THE GROWING POWER OF THE WHITES IS NEVER FAR FROM THE CLOUDED THOUGHTS OF THE COMANCHE CHIEFS. THEY NEED A WHITE LEADER THEY CAN TRUST, AND NEIGHBORS IS ONE OF THE FEW TO BE FOUND.

IF ANYBODY CAN HELP US, HE'S THE MAN!!

WISH THEY WERE ALL LIKE HIM.

IN 1847 NEIGHBORS LENDS HIS INFLUENCE TO THE NEW GERMAN COLONISTS IN MAKING A TREATY WITH THE PENATEKAS, STILL THE STRONGEST OF THE FADING SOUTHERN COMANCHE BANDS.

WE WISH TO COME LIVE AMONG YOU AS FRIENDS. WE DO NOT FEAR WAR, BUT PREFER PEACE, TO DWELL TOGETHER AS BROTHERS, ALL EQUAL — RED AND WHITE! WE DO NOT WISH TO DRIVE YOU FROM YOUR HUNTING GROUNDS...

THE PENATEKAS, WHOSE LEADERSHIP IS STILL IN DISARRAY FROM THE COUNCIL HOUSE AFFAIR, ARE REPRESENTED BY THREE VERY DIFFERENT PERSONALITIES. *OLD OWL*, THE POLITICAL CHIEF, IS A SMALL, INSIGNIFICANT LOOKING MAN IN HIS DIRTY COTTON JACKET, BUT HIS FACE IS CRAFTY AND DIPLOMATIC.

THE WAR CHIEF, *SANTA ANA*, IS A LARGE MAN, POWERFULLY BUILT, WITH A BENEVOLENT AND LIVELY EXPRESSION. JUST LAST YEAR HE WENT WITH A DELEGATION OF OTHER CHIEFS TO WASHINGTON WHERE HE MET THE 'GREAT WHITE FATHER' AND CAME AWAY AWED BY HIS JOURNEY.

BUT THE THIRD, *BUFFALO HUMP*, FAMED FOR HIS RAIDS AGAINST THE TEXANS, IS A LIVING INCARNATION OF THE 'MURDERING REDSKIN'. UNLIKE MOST OF HIS TRIBE, HE SCORNS EVEN THE WHITEMAN'S CLOTHES AND DRESSES IN PURE COMANCHE FASHION.

...WE WILL NEED BUT LITTLE OF THE LAND TO GROW OUR CROPS. *MUCH* WILL REMAIN FOR YOU, OUR BROTHERS.

MY PEOPLE KNOW HOW TO WIN FROM THE EARTH MANY THINGS THAT YOU LIKE TO EAT...

WHEN THE BUFFALO GO AND THE NORTH WIND SWEEPS DOWN, LEAVING YOU COLD AND HUNGRY, COME TO US AND WE WILL SHARE OUR FOOD WITH YOU...

THEY LISTEN CAREFULLY TO THE WORDS OF THIS STRANGE WHITE TRIBE, 'LOS ALEMANES' & THEIR CHIEF, MEUSEBACH, 'EL SOL COLORADO', FOR OF ALL THE ENCROACHING SETTLERS, THEY ARE THE ONLY ONES TO RECOGNIZE THAT REDMEN OWN THE LAND.

HE SAYS, "FOR THIS TREATY WE WILL GIVE YOU AND YOUR SQUAWS MANY PRESENTS AND OUR HEARTS WILL ALL BE GLAD. LET THERE BE NO STONES ON THE PATH BETWEEN US. LET THE EARTH, OUR COMMON MOTHER, WITNESS THAT MY WORDS TO YOU ARE TRUE."

GRUNT!

GRUNT!

THROUGH THE FORESIGHT OF THE GERMAN LEADERS, THEIR TINY SETTLEMENTS AROUND NEW BRAUNFELS AND FREDERICKSBURG ENJOY A TRUCE WITH THE COMANCHES, A PEACE MOSTLY KEPT BY BOTH SIDES, IN THE COMING YEARS OF BLOODSHED.

Velkommen, you vont bier?!

Alemán.. friend!!

PSST— DON'T FORGET TO ASK ABOUT SOME COFFEE!

BUT DESPITE THE GOOD INTENTIONS OF MEN LIKE MEUSEBACH AND NEIGHBORS, A STORM IS BREWING OVER TEXAS — A STORM OF SUCH INTENSITY THAT IT THREATENS TO SWEEP AWAY ALL PROGRESS MADE WITH THE REDMAN.

I SAY DAMN THAT INJUN-LOVER HOUSTON, HIS BOOT-LICKER, NEIGHBORS, AND ALL LIKE 'UM! IT'S THEM OR US!!

FOR THIS GATHERING TEMPEST, THIS DARK SPECTRE REARING ITS CAVERNOUS HEAD IN THE LAND IS GENOCIDE... RACE KILLING! LIKE THE HORSEMEN OF OLD — WAR, PESTILENCE, FAMINE — IT HERALDS A STRUGGLE TO THE FINISH, CRUEL, UGLY, WITHOUT PITY FOR THE YOUNG, THE WEAK, OR THE OLD — AND WITH ONLY ONE SURVIVOR!

IF WE COULD JUST SET ASIDE A PLACE FOR THEM, GIVE THEM A LITTLE BREATH-ING ROOM WHILE THEY LEARNED TO FARM..

ABOUT THIS TIME THE COMANCHES NOTICE THAT WAGONTRAINS ARE MOVING ACROSS THEIR LANDS, MINERS BOUND FOR THE CALIFORNIA GOLDFIELDS.

LODGES THAT MOVE STANDING UP..

JUST SO LONG AS THEY KEEP MOVING.

ITEMS DISCARDED AT THE EMIGRANTS' CAMPSITES SPREAD DISEASE AMONG THE BANDS ~ DREADED CHOLERA AND SMALLPOX.

IMAGINE ~ THROWING AWAY NEAT STUFF LIKE THIS! WHITE PEOPLE MUST BE CRAZY.

GIVE IT TO YOUR WIFE, WOLF ROBE. SHE'LL LOVE IT.

WONDER WHAT THEY HID IN THAT PILE OF ROCKS?

THE COMANCHES LOSE SANTA ANA AND OLD OWL, TWO OF THEIR MOST POWERFUL CHIEFS, AND THEIR NUMBERS ARE DECIMATED.

PETA VOWS TO SHUN ALL CONTACT WITH THE WHITES AND MOVES HIS PEOPLE AWAY FROM THE WAGON ROUTE ON THE CANADIAN RIVER.

ALL I KNOW IS IT DIDN'T HAPPEN BEFORE THOSE DRIFTERS SHOWED UP...

QUANAH GROWS AND IS SOON JOINED BY A BROTHER AND SISTER.

HIS CHILDHOOD IS A TIME OF CONFUSION AND UNCERTAINTY FOR THE COMANCHES. WARRIORS FROM OTHER BANDS, LIKE THE PENATEKAS, BRING BAD NEWS FROM THE TEXAS FRONTIER.

THEY WANT US TO LIVE ON A TINY RESERVATION — PENNED UP LIKE TAME CATTLE.

BUFFALO HUMP, JOIN US HERE. WE WILL BE FREE LIKE THE WIND!

NEVERTHELESS THE BOY LEARNS TO RIDE WITH ALL THE FLAIR OF HIS PEOPLE, WHO WORSHIP THE HORSE AS THE SACRED GOD-DOG.

FATHER—LOOK! THE GOD-DOG AND I ARE ONE!!

WHEN QUANAH IS 13, PETA NOCONA TAKES HIS BAND TO VISIT HIS FATHER POHEBITS-QUASHO, HEAD CHIEF OF ALL THE QUOHADAS, CAMPED HIGH ON THE CANADIAN RIVER.

MY SON, WHERE YOU BEEN ALL THIS TIME?

TRYING TO KEEP CLEAR OF THOSE PESKY WHITEFOLKS..

LOOKS LIKE YOU DIDN'T TRY TOO HARD WHEN IT CAME TO THEIR WOMEN! AND WHO'S THIS, EH?

MY NUMBER ONE SON — QUANAH!

OLD POHEBITS-QUASHO IS PLEASED WITH HIS GRANDSON, AND AFTER COMANCHE CUSTOM, TAKES A GUIDING HAND IN HIS TRAINING.

IF YOU'RE GONNA BE A COMANCHE SON, YOU GOTTA HAVE A HORSE..

WOW!

HE SHOWS HIM HOW TO KILL THE BUFFALO...

SEE? NOW AIM BEHIND THE LAST RIB AND YOUR ARROW WILL PENETRATE HIS HEART!

...AND TO RELISH THE TASTE OF THE *LIVER*, YANKED STEAMING FROM THE FALLEN BEAST.

HERE.. SPRINKLE SOME GALL ON IT.. TASTES TWICE AS GOOD!

TO WAIT IN A BAITED PIT AND CATCH THE EAGLE FOR ITS FEATHERS.

ONE GRAB IS ALL YOU GET, SO MAKE IT COUNT..

HE TEACHES QUANAH TO MAKE WEAPONS — KNIVES, CLUBS, SPEARS, BOWS AND ARROWS — TOOLS OF SURVIVAL FOR THE COMANCHE WAY OF LIFE.

NOW IF YOU HAD YOU A *SWEETHEART*, SHE COULD PUT SOME NICE BEADWORK ON THERE FOR YOU, EH?

NO PROBLEM.. I GOT PLENTY OF SWEETHEARTS..

AND TELLS HIM ABOUT *MEDICINE*.

SOMEDAY, WHEN YOU BE-GIN TO KNOW WHO YOU ARE, YOU WILL SEEK A *VISION*, AND IT WILL TELL YOU WHAT YOU MUST DO TO BE STRONG IN BATTLE.

WHAT DID IT *YOU* TELL, GRANDPA?

IT TOLD ME TO WEAR THIS JACKET OF IRON, THAT MAKES MY ENEMIES' ARROWS BOUNCE OFF LIKE HAIL ON A TEPEE!!

32

IT IS PEACEFUL THIS MAY OF 1858 AS THE COMBINED BANDS OF PETA NOCONA AND POHEBITS QUASHO ARE CAMPED IN THE ANTELOPE HILLS. BUT IT IS NOT PEACEFUL IN TEXAS WHERE THE SETTLERS ARE SUFFERING FROM ATTACKS AT THE HANDS OF THE DESPERATE PENA-TEKAS. COL. JOHN S. (RIP) FORD AND 100 RANGERS, AIDED BY CHIEF PLACIDO AND 100 TONKAWA BRAVES, ARE ORDERED TO STANCH THE WOUNDS OF THE BLEEDING FRONTIER BY GIVING BATTLE TO THE COMANCHES IN THEIR OWN STRONGHOLDS.

I DON'T LIKE THEM DAMN INJUNS ANY MORE THAN YOU DO, COL. JOHN.

POINT THAT THING THE OTHER WAY, WILL YA CHIEF? MAKES ME NERVOUS AS HELL.

THE TONKAWAS ARE ESPECIALLY HATED BY THE COMANCHES, NOT ONLY BECAUSE THEY LEAD THEIR ENEMIES AGAINST THEM, BUT BECAUSE THEY EAT THE FLESH OF THEIR VANQUISHED FOES.

..IRON JACKET'S VILLAGE..

AS THE ALARM IS SPREAD, POHEBITS-QUASHO RESOLVES TO PUNISH THE AUDACITY OF THESE WHITEMEN WHO VIOLATE HIS TERRITORY.

THEY GOT A LOT OF NERVE, BUSTING IN HERE LIKE THIS!

HE MOUNTS AND PARADES HIS INVUNERABILITY BEFORE THE GATHERED TROOPS.

HEY HEY, YOU POSSUM LOVERS, COME OUT AND FIGHT IRON JACKET!!

TIME AND TIME AGAIN THE FEARLESS OLD WARRIOR STREAKS DOWN THE TEXAN LINE, SEEMINGLY OBLIVIOUS TO THEIR RAIN OF FIRE.

DARN! I COULD HAVE SWORN I HIT HIM SMACK-DAB IN THE CHEST!

IRON JACKET HAVE HEAP MEDICINE. NO CAN KILL...

BUT ONE TONKAWA WARRIOR'S AIM IS MORE PRECISE. POHEBITS-QUASHO, HIT IN THE NECK, FALLS FROM HIS HORSE IN A HEAP.

MAYBE SO, JACKET OF IRON, BUT HEAD JUST PLAIN BONE...

ALRIGHT BOYS, MOUNT UP!

THEIR INVINCIBLE CHIEF DEAD, THE ASTONISHED WARRIORS FALL BACK IN DISMAY, AND FORD'S TROOPS CHARGE INTO THE EXPOSED VILLAGE.

ON A DISTANT HILL, PETA NOCONA VIEWS THE DESTRUCTION OF HIS FATHER'S VILLAGE.

GO BACK, TELL THE WOMEN TO **PACK UP!** I'LL HOLD THEM OFF AS LONG AS I CAN. QUANAH, GO WITH YOUR MOTHER!!

PETA'S WARRIORS, IN A RUNNING FIGHT, MANAGE TO HOLD THE TEXANS AT BAY WHILE THE VILLAGES FURTHER DOWN THE CANADIAN EVACUATE.

LATER, AFTER FORD'S VICTORIOUS FORCE WITHDRAWS, PETA SEARCHES THE BATTLEFIELD FOR HIS SLAIN FATHER'S BODY.

HOW CRUEL IT WILL BE FOR YOU, MY SON, TO DO BATTLE FOR **MY** PEOPLE AGAINST THE PEOPLE OF YOUR **MOTHER.** HALF OF YOU WILL WIN, BUT THE OTHER HALF MUST ALWAYS **LOSE..**

NOW I AM CHIEF OF THE QUOHADAS. **HEAR ME,** SPIRIT OF MY DE-FILED FATHER— YOU WILL BE **AVENGED!!** BLOOD WILL COV-ER THE MOON!

BUT LATER THAT YEAR, BUFFALO HUMP AND HIS PENATEKAS ARE HIT BY ANOTHER TEXAN ARMY..

WIPED OUT.. EVERYTHING **GONE**, PETA. HORSES, CAMP GEAR, TEEPEES, OUR FOOD SUPPLY — WE NEVER HAD A **CHANCE**.. THOSE DAMN TEXANS ARE LIKE BLOWFLIES.

DON'T WORRY. WE'LL RAID DOWN **SOUTH** AND GET YOU BACK IN THE SADDLE AGAIN.

AND SO, AT THE NEXT FULL MOON, LONG-SUFFERING MEXICO PAYS FOR COMANCHE LOSSES AT THE HANDS OF MILITANT TEXANS...

IT IS A TIME-HONORED PRACTICE WHICH THE COMANCHES REFER TO AS "THE MEXICAN WAR".

GOING TO THE **BENT BROTHERS'** FORT, HIGH IN THE STAKED PLAINS, PETA AND BUFFALO HUMP TRY TO BARTER THEIR LOOT.

HE SAYS HIS GOVERNMENT WON'T LET HIM BUY MEXICAN STUFF. THEY'RE **FRIENDS** NOW..

SO WHAT?? WE'LL DEAL WITH THE **COMANCHEROS!**

A BRISK TRADE GROWS BETWEEN THEM AND THE OUT-CAST COMANCHEROS, WHO HAVE **NO QUALMS** ABOUT THE SOURCE OF MERCHANDISE.

MEXICAN, TEXAN.. IT'S ALL THE SAME TO US.

MEANWHILE, ON THE TWO LITTLE RESERVATIONS ESTABLISHED IN 1855, EVENTS ARE COMING TO A HEAD. ALTHO THE PEACEFUL TEXAS TRIBES, AND SOME PENATEKAS, ARE MAKING FAIR PROGRESS AT ADOPTING THE 'WHITEMAN'S ROAD,' LOCAL MALCONTENTS ARE WORKING OVERTIME TO PLOT THEIR DESTRUCTION.

THESE MELONS AND SQUASH LOOK REAL GOOD, WIFE!

YEAH...IF THE WHITES DON'T STEAL IT ALL.

JOHN R. BAYLOR, A FORMER INDIAN AGENT, HARBORS BITTER HATRED TOWARD NEIGHBORS FOR HIS DISMISSAL. HE KEEPS THE SETTLERS STIRRED UP AGAINST THE AGENT AND HIS CHARGES.

IT'S ALL HERE IN MY PAPER — STORIES THAT'LL MAKE YOUR BLOOD CURDLE. THOSE RESERVE INDIANS ARE TO BLAME, AND NEIGHBORS IS THE WORST! WE SHOULD DRIVE THEM OUT!

THE WHITE MAN

RAPED   LOOTED   KILLED

BURNED

SCALPED

IRONICALLY, THE RESERVE INDIANS OFTEN RIDE BESIDE TEXAN LEADERS LIKE RIP FORD AND SUL ROSS IN THEIR CAMPAIGNS AGAINST THE HOSTILE NORTHERN BANDS, RENDERING VALUABLE SERVICE IN DEFENSE OF THE FRONTIER.

WHY NOT ?? THOSE CRAZIES GIVE US MORE TROUBLE THAN ANYBODY!

AGENT NEIGHBORS AND CAPT. SHAPLEY ROSS, SUL'S FATHER AND ALSO AN AGENT, STAND ALONE AGAINST THE RABBLE. EVEN THEIR FRIEND, 'OLD RIP,' WILL NOT HELP IF IT MEANS BRINGING WHITEMEN IN FOR CRIMES AGAINST REDMEN.

AS SENIOR RANGER, IT'S YOUR DUTY TO BRING THOSE MURDERERS TO JUSTICE.

DUTY, HELL !! YOU KNOW AS WELL AS I DO, ROBERT, THAT IF I ARREST THOSE MEN, TH' WHOLE DERN COUNTRY WILL ERUPT IN A CIVIL WAR!

I HATE TO ADMIT IT, BUT HE'S RIGHT...

BUT BAYLOR, UNABLE TO DISCREDIT AND OUST NEIGHBORS LEGITIMATELY, WILL NOT DESIST. HE GATHERS AN ARMED MOB AND THREATENS TO FORCEABLY BREAK UP THE RESERVE — WHILE MOST OF ITS WARRIORS ARE OFF HELPING VAN DORN DEFEAT BUFFALO HUMP! ONLY THE BOLD STANCE OF A FEW BRAVES UNDER ANADARKO CHIEF JOSÉ MARÍA, BACKED BY CAPT. ROSS AND A SMALL CONTINGENT OF SOLDIERS, KEEPS BAYLOR FROM HIS FOND DREAM OF AN INDIAN BLOODBATH.

COME ON, YOU YELLOW-BELLIES !! WE'LL SHOW YOU THAT EVEN PEACEFUL INDIANS HAVE GOT SOME FIGHT LEFT!

HOLD YOUR FIRE MEN, UNTIL FIRED UPON...

HMM...MAYBE THIS WASN'T SUCH A GOOD IDEA...

THAT SAME YEAR SEES THE TEXANS DISMANTLE THEIR RESERVATION SYSTEM AND DRIVE ALL FRIENDLY INDIANS BEYOND THEIR BORDERS.

THIS IS THE THANKS WE GET FOR BEING *GOOD* INDIANS..

UPON HIS RETURN FROM THIS UNPLEASANT DUTY, AGENT NEIGHBORS, DEDICATED PUBLIC SERVANT AND PATRIOT OF TEXAS, IS OPENLY *MURDERED* ON THE STREETS OF BELKNAP.

MANY OF THE COMANCHES ESCAPE IN DESTITUTION TO THEIR COUSINS ON THE PLAINS RATHER THAN BE HERDED INTO INDIAN TERRITORY.

THEY HAVE TAKEN *EVERY-THING* FROM US. ALL THEIR PAPER TREATIES MEANT *NOTHING*. WE PENATEKAS ARE A BROKEN PEOPLE.

PETA, DISTURBED AT THE BROKEN PROMISES AND THE WHITES' ABILITY TO STRIKE WITH EASE DEEP INTO TRADITIONAL COMANCHE LAND, DECIDES TO SHIFT HIS RAIDS BACK TO THE TEXAS FRONTIER BEFORE IT IS TOO LATE.

..NOW THEY WILL *PAY*... FATHER !

HE MOVES HIS CAMP TO THE PEASE RIVER COUNTRY TO BE CLOSER TO HIS TARGETS.

THAT FALL, PARKER COUNTY IS ABLAZE WITH HIS VENGEANCE. LITTLE DOES PETA NOCONA SUSPECT THAT MANY OF HIS VICTIMS ARE THE FRIENDS AND NEIGHBORS OF HIS OWN WIFE'S FAMILY.

THE SETTLERS CLAMOR TO THE AUTHORITIES FOR PROTECTION. A MIXED FORCE OF VOLUNTEERS, RANGERS, TONKAWA SCOUTS, AND ARMY REGULARS, ALL UNDER YOUNG CAPT. SUL ROSS, IS RAISED TO PURSUE THE RAIDERS.

YOU'RE A SORRY-LOOKIN' BUNCH, BUT YOU'RE THE BEST WE GOT..

YOUNG WHIPPER-SNAPPER

PETA, AWARE OF THE HORNET'S NEST HE HAS STIRRED UP, TAKES HIS SPOILS AND HEADS WEST, KEEPING HIS BAND ON THE MOVE, STOPPING ONLY TO KILL FRESH MEAT UNTIL HE FEELS **SAFE**.

THERE'S A HERD UP THE RIVER. WE'LL GO HUNT NOW, AND COME ON BACK TOMORROW..

WHILE PETA'S WARRIORS ARE OFF HUNTING, ROSS CATCHES UP WITH THEIR CAMP, CONTAINING WOMEN, CHILDREN, AND MEXICAN 'SLAVES.'

CAPT. ROSS SPOTS A WARRIOR TRYING TO GET AWAY WITH SEVERAL WOMEN.. THE SCOURGE OF THE FRONTIER, TURNING TAIL AND RUNNING!

ROSS PURSUES AND FIRES, KILLING THE GIRL RIDING DOUBLE. ONLY THE TOUGH, BULLHIDE SHIELD SLUNG ON HIS BACK SAVES HIM FROM DEATH.

YOU WON'T GET OFF THIS EASY, NOCONA..

DON'T SHOOT THAT ONE! IT'S A WHITE WOMAN!

TUMBLING FROM HIS HORSE, THE WARRIOR NIMBLY REGAINS HIS FEET AND PUTS AN ARROW INTO ROSS' MOUNT BEFORE HE IS SHOT DOWN.

THE WOMAN! DON'T LET HER GET AWAY!!

THE WARRIOR, REALIZING HE IS FINISHED, STAGGERS TO A MESQUITE TREE AND BEGINS HIS COMANCHE DEATH SONG.

TELL HIM IN SPAN-ISH TO SURRENDER, MARTINEZ.

UNKNOWN TO ROSS, THE HEROIC WARRIOR IS NOT PETA NOCONA, BUT THE CHIEF'S FAITHFUL MEXICAN SLAVE, WHO DIES TRYING TO PROTECT HIS MASTER'S WIFE AND HELP HER ESCAPE CAPTURE.

PUT HIM OUT OF HIS MISERY, BOYS..

MEANWHILE, NADUAH AND HER LITTLE DAUGHTER, TOP-SANNAH, ARE CAUGHT AND LED BACK TO THE CAMP.

YOU WUZ RIGHT, CAPTAIN—IT'S A WHITE WOMAN, BY GUM. I'LL BETCHA THIS IS TH' PARKER GIRL WE KEEP HEARIN' ABOUT.

CONVINCED THEY HAVE DESTROYED PETA NOCONA, ROSS AND HIS MEN LEAVE, TAKING THE RECAPTURED BOOTY AND THE WHITE COMANCHE WOMAN.

THAT'S THE END OF THAT RASCAL...

WHEN PETA AND HIS WARRIORS RETURN, A SCENE OF **DESOLATION** GREETS THEM. A SURVIVOR TELLS THE SAD TALE. PETA, NEVER DREAMING THAT THE WHITEMAN WOULD DARE CHASE THEM TO THE HEART OF THE BISON RANGE, IS PLUNGED INTO TERRIBLE **GRIEF**.

IT IS A SHAKEN GROUP OF WARRIORS THAT RETREAT TO THE STAKED PLAINS THIS DECEMBER, THEIR FAMILIES **DEAD** OR SCATTERED, THEIR WEALTH CONFISCATED OR DESTROYED BY THE HATED TEXANS.

CHIEF PETA NOCONA IS HEARTBROKEN OVER THE LOSS OF NADUAH. HE REFUSES TO TAKE ANOTHER WIFE, AND BECOMES MOODY AND FATALISTIC.

CYNTHIA ANN'S
SECOND CAPTIVITY

CAPT. SUL ROSS, CERTAIN THAT THE CAPTURED WHITE COMANCHE WOMAN IS THE LONG-LOST CYNTHIA ANN PARKER, TAKES HER TO CAMP COOPER, AN OUTPOST NEAR THE VACANT BRAZOS INDIAN RESERVATION.

SHE AND HER 18 MONTH OLD DAUGHTER, TOPSANNAH, ARE BATHED, GIVEN CLOTHES, AND REASSURED BY THE POST WOMEN.

NOW DON'T BE AFRAID, HONEY.. WE WON'T HURT YOU.

POOR THING..

ROSS SENDS FOR COL. ISAAC PARKER, AND THROUGH A MEXICAN INTERPRETER, THEY VAINLY ATTEMPT TO BREAK THROUGH NADUAH'S STOLID EXPRESSION AND AWAKEN OLD MEMORIES.

IT MIGHT BE HER.. MAYBE WE ARE WRONG. POOR CYNTHIA ANN..

AT THE SOUND OF HER **LONG-FORGOTTEN NAME**, A SPARK OF LIFE ANIMATES NADUAH'S LISTLESS EYES.

CYNTHIA.. CYNTHIA ANN!

COL. PARKER IS SATISFIED OF HIS NIECE'S IDENTITY. SHE AND HER CHILD ARE JOYFULLY RECEIVED BACK BY THE PARKER CLAN.

DON'T WORRY, CHILD. WE'LL TAKE CARE OF YOU... AFTER ALL, YOU'RE A PARKER.

BUT AFTER 25 YEARS OF COMANCHE LIFE, CYNTHIA ANN IS **MORE INDIAN** THAN **WHITE**. SHE MOURNS HER LOST LOVED ONES COMANCHE FASHION, MUCH TO THE HORROR OF HER CIVILIZED RELATIVES.

CYNTHIA ANN.. WHAT???— OH MY GOD!!

TOBACCO

SHE TRIES TO ESCAPE BACK TO HER **FAMILY** —AND THE ONLY PEOPLE SHE KNOWS— EVERY TIME SHE CAN STEAL A HORSE.

IT'S HOPELESS. WE'LL HAVE TO WATCH HER CONSTANTLY..

THE PARKERS TAKE HER TO AUSTIN WHERE THE STATE **LEGIS-LATURE** GRANTS HER A LEAGUE OF LAND AND AN ANNUAL PENSION OF $100 TO EASE HER DIFFICULT RETURN TO CIVILIZATION.

SHE THINKS THEY'RE A WAR COUNCIL, DECIDING ON HER FATE.

SINCE SHE SEEMED SO UNHAPPY WITH HER UNCLE ISAAC AT BIRD-VILLE, HER BROTHER SILAS JR. AGREES TO TAKE HER INTO HER CARE.

THEY'RE GONE, CYNTHIA, YOU MUST ACCEPT IT AND LET US HELP YOU START A NEW LIFE..

MY HUSBAND, SONS..

CYNTHIA QUICKLY PICKS UP THE PIONEER SKILLS OF PLAITING, SPINNING, AND WEAVING THAT ARE CONSTANTLY REQUIRED OF SOUTH-ERN WHITE WOMEN DURING THE LEAN CIVIL WAR YEARS.

I DECLARE, CYNTHIA, YOU CAN DO ANYTHING YOU SET YOUR MIND TO!

NO STRANGER TO HARD WORK, SHE PROVES TO BE AN INDUSTRIOUS ADDITION TO THE PARKER CLAN.

SHE CAN USE AN AXE GOOD AS MOST MEN.

LITTLE TOPSANNAH, CALLED "TECKS ANN" BY HER NEW VAN ZANDT COUNTY NEIGHBORS, IS A BRIGHT AND PRETTY CHILD.

BABY SEZ IT HONGRY..

LISTEN AT THAT— TALKS ENGLISH BETTER THAN HER MOMMA!

WHEN A FEVER TAKES THE GIRL, HER MOTHER'S ONLY RAY OF SUNSHINE, CYNTHIA IS INCONSOLABLE AND SINKS INTO A DEEP APATHY.

CYNTHIA, EAT SOMETHING, HONEY... YOU'LL STARVE YOUR-SELF LIKE THIS...

HER ONLY DESIRE IS TO GO BACK AND TRY TO FIND HER HUSBAND AND TWO SONS, IF THEY ARE STILL ALIVE ON THE PLAINS.

AFTER THE WAR, WE'LL TAKE YOU BACK TO THE COMANCHES, IF THAT'S WHAT YOU WANT, BUT YOU'VE GOT TO KEEP YOUR STRENGTH UP, CHILD.

BUT THE WAR DRAGS ON, AND CYNTHIA DESPAIRS, HER EYES FIXED IN A FATHOMLESS GAZE ON THE PRAIRIES, FAR BEYOND THE PINEY WOODS, AS IF SEARCHING FOR HER LOST HAPPINESS.

WON'T STIR, WON'T EAT, NEVER SMILES— I JUST DON'T KNOW..

FINALLY SHE DIES OF A **BROKEN HEART** AND IS BURIED BESIDE HER LITTLE TOPSANNAH..

WHILE DEEP IN THE PLAINS, EACH TIME THE ORPHAN **QUANAH** BREATHES THE FRAGRANCE OF HIS NAMESAKE, THE BLOSSOMING WILDFLOWERS, HIS THOUGHTS WANDER TO HIS BELOVED MOTHER.

NADUAH, I WONDER WHERE YOU ARE NOW.

SEVERAL YEARS LATER, PETA NOCONA, WHO NEVER RECOVERS FROM THE LOSS OF HIS FAIR NADUAH, DIES OF AN INFECTED WOUND, LEAVING HIS TWO ORPHANED SONS TO FEND FOR THEMSELVES.

WITH THEIR DYNAMIC LEADER GONE, MANY NOCONIS DRIFT AWAY TO JOIN OTHER BANDS. ALTHO THE NOCONI BAND REMAINS INTACT, ITS INFLUENCE IS HENCEFORTH TO BE ECLIPSED BY THE FIERCE **QUOHADAS**, MASTERS OF THE STAKED PLAINS!

WITHOUT PETA THINGS JUST WON'T BE THE SAME...

VISION SEEKER

QUANAH, AS THE UNTRIED SON OF A FAMED CHIEF, FACES AN UNCERTAIN FUTURE WITH THE QUOHADAS. THEY WELCOME HIM BECAUSE OF HIS FATHER'S MEMORY, BUT SOME FEAR HIM AS A POTENTIAL THREAT TO THEIR OWN POWER.

YOUR FATHER WAS A BOLD AND COURAGEOUS MAN, A TRUE QUOHADA. STAY WITH US...

BUT WATCH YOURSELF, KID.

YOUNG PECOS, NEVER A STURDY CHILD, BECOMES ILL AND QUICKLY DIES OF A MYSTERIOUS 'DISEASE'.

POOR LITTLE BROTHER.. YOU NEVER HAD A CHANCE..

SO QUANAH STANDS ALONE, CONFUSED AND BITTER, CERTAIN ONLY OF HIS HATRED FOR THE WHITES, WHOSE COMING SEEMS TO HAVE CAST A DARK SHADOW OVER HIS LIFE.

IN AN EARLIER TIME HE WOULD BE HEIR TO WEALTH AND POWER, SURROUNDED BY A STRONG, PROTECTIVE CLAN — A PRINCE BY HIS WORLD'S STANDARDS. NOW HE IS BUT AN OUTCAST, LIVING OFF THE CRUMBS OF GENEROSITY IN THE MIDST OF SUSPICION. QUANAH BROODS, PONDERING THE CRUEL TURN OF FATE THAT HAS STRIPPED HIM OF HIS BIRTHRIGHT.

THEN HE REMEMBERS THE WORDS OF HIS GRANDFATHER, IRON JACKET, SPOKEN, NOW IT SEEMS, SO LONG AGO...

SOMEDAY... WHEN YOU BEGIN TO KNOW WHO YOU ARE, YOU WILL SEEK A VISION...

SUDDENLY, HIS PATHWAY BECOMES CLEAR.

IT IS TIME, UNCLE, THAT I KNEW THE WILL OF THE GREAT SPIRIT.

SO QUANAH SETS ABOUT TO PURIFY HIMSELF FOR HIS QUEST.

ENTER THE LODGE, MY SON. THE STONES ARE HOT.. WE MAY BEGIN.

AS STEAM RISES FROM WATER SPRINKLED ON THE HOT ROCKS, QUANAH CHANTS AND RUBS HIS BODY WITH SAGE.

HE EMERGES FROM THE SWEAT LODGE, CLEANSED OF BODILY POISONS.

CLAD ONLY IN BREECHCLOUT AND MOCCASINS, THE YOUTH IS GIVEN A BONE PIPE, TOBACCO, AND A NEWLY PREPARED BUFFALO ROBE, RUBBED WITH WHITE CLAY TO SYMBOLIZE PURITY.

HUH YIYI YUH HI YIYI HUH

ALONE HE MAKES HIS WAY TO A DISTANT HILL, RICH IN COMANCHE LORE AS THE ABODE OF POWERFUL SPIRIT FORCES. HE CHOOSES A SPOT WHERE HE CAN SEE THE RISING AND SETTING OF THE SUN. AS DARKNESS APPROACHES, THE SUPPLIANT SMOKES AND PRAYS FOR POWER — POWER TO KNOW HIMSELF, AND THE POWER TO USE HIS KNOWLEDGE FOR GOOD.

THAT NIGHT QUANAH COVERS HIMSELF, FACING EAST— TRYING IN VAIN TO SWEEP THE TURMOIL FROM HIS MIND, SO THAT THE SPIRIT DIMENSION MAY FREELY ENTER.

RISING AT DAYBREAK, HE POSITIONS HIMSELF TO RECEIVE THE STRENGTH RADIATING FROM THE NEWBORN SUN.

BUT THE DAY SLIPS AWAY, WITH NO SIGN FROM THE SPIRIT WORLD...

AND THE NEXT DAY, STILL NOTHING TO BREAK HIS LONELY VIGIL...

....?

AND THE NEXT, AGAIN NOTHING, THO EVERY NERVE STRAINS TO THE LIMIT.

ANTS, CRAWLING ON MY LEG...SOME MEANING, PERHAPS?

WEAK FROM FASTING, TROUBLED OF MIND, QUANAH LAYS DOWN AGAIN ON HIS BED OF SAGE, DOUBTS CROWDING IN.

COULD IT BE THAT YOU CHOOSE ONLY TO SPEAK TO ME THRU GNATS AND BUGS? OH GREAT FATHER, AM I SO UNWORTHY??

BUT THE ONLY ANSWER TO HIS SOUL-SEARCHING IS THE DISMAL WAIL OF A COYOTE, THE SLY JESTER OF COMANCHE MYTH.

49

ON THE FORTH DAY QUANAH STRUGGLES TO REMAIN ALERT. THE SUN SEEMS TO PULSE LIKE A LIVING THING, THROBBING, FLOWING OVER, OBLITERATING HIM. HIS EARS RING.

SUDDENLY, THERE IS A CRASHING SOUND — LIKE THE UNIVERSE BEING SPLIT ASUNDER — THE SWISHING OF WINGS, A SWIRL OF MOTION, BLINDING LIGHT, AND THEN, TOTAL SILENCE.

IT..IS..NO USE!

WHEN QUANAH OPENS HIS EYES, BEFORE HIM SITS AN APPARITION, REAL AS THE DUST SETTLING ON HIS DAMP BROW — A WINGED BISON, WHITE AS THE DRIVEN SNOW... WITH SMALL, PINK EYES...

..BENEVOLENT EYES, TWINKLING WITH KINDLY AMUSEMENT..

LITTLE BROTHER, I HAVE A MESSAGE FOR YOU, FROM THE FATHER OF ALL..

BUT BEFORE THE DREAM-BEAST CAN SAY ANOTHER WORD, IT IS STRUCK BY A DAZZLING BOLT OF LIGHTNING!

50

AND DISSOLVES INTO A SMOLDERING, MAGGOT-INFESTED CARCASS.

QUANAH HEARS A DEAFENING, BUZZING NOISE, PEERS CLOSELY AND REALIZES THAT THE WRITHING MASS IS COMPOSED NOT OF WORMS, BUT BEES, SWARMING OVER A HUGE HONEYCOMB!

BUZZZZZZ

!

HERE, EAT OF MY BODY AND KNOW THAT FROM DECAY COMES NEW LIFE, THAT WHAT SEEMS TO BE ROTTEN AND PUTRID IS SWEET LIKE HONEY FOR THOSE THAT **DARE TO TASTE..**

HOLD CLOSE THIS TRUTH, AND I WILL NOT ABANDON YOU TO YOUR ENEMIES, THOUGH THEY SWARM ABOUT YOU LIKE A HIVE OF ANGRY BEES...

BUZZZZ

AGAIN THE BUZZING, THE SOUND OF COUNTLESS PAIRS OF BEATING WINGS — NO, IT IS ONLY THE BISON, FLYING OFF AGAIN INTO THE SUN.. FAR AWAY.. SLIPPING INTO OBLIVION...

WHEN QUANAH AWAKENS, IT IS TO THE FAINTLY-HEARD SOUND OF THUNDER AND THE FEEL OF GENTLE RAIN, SOOTHING HIS FEVERED SKIN. THE QUEST IS OVER.

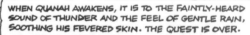

WEAKENED PHYSICALLY BUT EXHILARATED SPIRITUALLY, QUANAH SLOWLY MAKES HIS WAY BACK TO THE CAMP. STRANGE HOW *NEW* EVERYTHING SEEMS — EVERY BUSH, BLADE OF GRASS, EVEN THE ROCKS SING WITH A LIFE HE NEVER KNEW EXISTED.

AS HE NEARS THE CAMP, CRIERS CIRCULATE WORD OF HIS RETURN. CURIOUS EYES BEHOLD THE GAUNT SEEKER OF VISIONS, COME BACK FROM HIS HOLY QUEST. BUT IN THOSE EYES IS ALSO *RESPECT*, FOR AS ALL COMANCHES KNOW, WITHOUT A VISION A MAN IS NEXT TO NOTHING, WITH NO SOURCE OF POWER, NO SPECIAL WISDOM, AND NO PROTECTION.

AND HOW COULD THE COMANCHES PROSPER AS A PEOPLE UNLESS THEIR YOUNG MEN WALKED WITH THE SPIRITS THAT RULED THE ELEMENTS? *UNTHINKABLE!* THEREFORE, WELCOME THIS SEEKER BACK WITH RE-JOICING, AND HOPE THAT HE HAS RECEIVED STRONG MEDICINE, FOR *HIS* PERSONAL STRENGTH ADDS TO *OURS* AND MAKES US STRONG AS WELL!

IN THE DAYS TO COME, QUANAH QUIETLY GOES ABOUT GATH-ERING THE ARTICLES NEEDED TO FILL HIS **MEDICINE BUNDLE.** SOME TANGIBLE PART OF EVERY EARTHLY THING SEEN IN THE VISION IS ESSENTIAL, FOR HIS SPIRITUAL HELPERS MUST BE PROVIDED **ACTUAL DWELLING PLACES,** LEST THEY LEAVE AND TAKE THEIR POWER WITH THEM.

A SMOOTH, ROUND, TRANSLUCENT ROCK, A BIT OF DRIED HONEYCOMB, SPLINTERS OF A TREE STRUCK BY LIGHTNING, A BONE FRAGMENT OF A BUFFALO SAID TO BE PURE WHITE — ALL CAREFULLY WRAPPED IN SPECIALLY PREPARED SKINS.

AND THEN HE STARTS WORK ON HIS **SHIELD,** PAINTING ON ITS SURFACE THE PICTOGRAPHIC ELEMENTS OF HIS VISION — FOR IT IS THIS **REPRESENTATION,** NOT THE SHIELD ITSELF, THAT PROTECTS ITS BEARER AND LENDS HIM STRENGTH.

AT LAST QUANAH IS READY TO FORMALLY SHARE HIS EXPERIENCE WITH THE TRIBAL ELDERS. AFTER HE HAS SHOWN THEM HIS SHIELD AND DESCRIBED THE VISION, THE SHAMANS GIVE THEIR INTERPRETATIONS OF ITS MEANING.

THEY ARE AWED BY THE DEPTH OF HIS VISION, AND QUANAH IS CONSIDERED FORTUNATE TO HAVE BEEN SHOWN SUCH A SWEEP-ING MYSTERY. **WILD HORSE,** AN IMPORTANT CHIEF, GIVES HIM A SACRED AMULET TO ADORN HIS NEW WAR SHIELD — A TAIL SWITCH TAKEN FROM A REAL **ALBINO BISON!** THE BAND MURMURS ITS APPROVAL AND DEPARTS WELL SATISFIED.

BUT A VISION IS OF NO USE UNLESS ONE USES IT— AND IS USED **BY IT**. IT IS TIME FOR QUANAH TO TEST THE STRENGTH OF HIS MEDICINE. HE JOINS WITH OTHER RESTLESS YOUNG BRAVES, EAGER TO PERFORM FEATS OF BRAVERY, EAGER TO GAIN WEALTH AND MAKE REPUTATIONS FOR THEMSELVES AS UNTRIED COMANCHE YOUTHS ALWAYS HAVE — BY **WAR!**

RED RAIDER

THEY ORGANIZE SMALL RAIDS AND HORSE STEALING EXPEDITIONS. BASED ON THEIR RELATIVE SUCCESS, LEADERS START TO EMERGE.

IT AIN'T **MUCH**·· BUT IT'S A START.

IN A SHORT TIME, THE YOUNG MEN HAVE ESTABLISHED A TIGHT CADRE, WHERE EACH MEMBER'S ROLE IS MUTUALLY UNDERSTOOD.

OKAY·· ESA, YOU HANDLE THE BACK-UP CAMP·· KOBAY WILL TAKE THE ADVANCE SCOUT POSITION··

THE RAIDERS QUICKLY PICK UP ON THE FINE POINTS OF THE COMANCHES' FAVORITE FORM OF CAPITALISTIC ENTERPRISE — **STEALING THE BEST HORSES** THEY CAN GET THEIR HANDS ON.

A MAN'S WORTH HAS ALWAYS BEEN MEASURED BY HIS PONY-HERD. THUS IT HAS BEEN SINCE THE SACRED **GOD-DOG**, THE TITAN OF BEASTS OF BURDEN, WAS FIRST MASTERED BY COMANCHE.

TO THEM IT IS THE STANDARD UNIT OF CURRENCY. ANYTHING WORTH HAVING IN THEIR WORLD CAN BE OBTAINED BY THE MAN WHO HAS HORSES — AND THE POWER TO GET MORE.

GRADUALLY, THE MOST PROMISING YOUNG BRAVES ARE INVITED ON MORE **SERIOUS FORAYS** BY THE WARRIORS OF THE BAND — THE ONES WHO **ALREADY HAVE** COUPS AND HONORS.

..THOUGHT YOU MIGHT WANT TO COME ALONG.. UNLESS YOU'VE GOT SOMETHING BETTER TO DO.

THE WAY THE NEW RECRUITS CARRY THEMSELVES ON THE WAR TRAIL IS CAREFULLY SCRUTINIZED BY THEIR ELDERS.

THEY RANGE FAR ON ALL FRONTIERS OF THEIR DOMAIN, CONSTANTLY TESTING THEIR ENEMIES' STRENGTHS AND WEAKNESSES, GATHERING ALL THE BOOTY THEY CAN WREST FROM THEM, WITH THE **LEAST POSSIBLE DAMAGE TO THEMSELVES.**

TONKAWA SCOUTS..

A COMANCHE DOES NOT GAIN SUCCESS AS A **LEADER** IF HE LOSES MEN ON THE WARPATH. THE SMART MAN IS THE ONE WHO GAINS THE PRIZE — AND **LIVES** TO TELL THE TALE.

WAIT A MINUTE!! SOMETHING'S GOING ON DOWN THERE!

YIYIYIIIEE

HEY, THAT'S **LOUD TALKER.** WHAT'S HE DOING!?!

EXCESSIVELY RECKLESS, FOOLHARDY BEHAVIOR IS **NOT** ENCOURAGED IN THE YOUNG BRAVES, FOR IT ENDANGERS THE SUCCESS OF THE VENTURE AND THE SAFETY OF ALL.

HE'S SUPPOSED TO BE GUARDING THE EXIT WITH QUANAH.

THE IDIOT! HE'LL RUIN EVERYTHING!

NEVERTHELESS, ONCE THE DIE IS CAST, A COMANCHE WOULD RISK EVERYTHING TO PREVENT THE BODY OF A SLAIN COMRADE, NO MATTER HOW **STUPID,** FROM FALLING INTO THE HANDS OF AN **ENEMY** — ESPECIALLY AN ENEMY LIKE THE FOUL TONKAWAS.

COMANCHES!! FOR **THIS** LIFE AND THE NEXT — DEATH TO THE FLESH EATERS!

FOR IT IS A TONKAWA RELIGIOUS PRACTICE TO **EAT PARTS** OF THEIR VICTIMS' BODIES. SINCE THE COMANCHES BELIEVE THAT MUTILATION AFTER DEATH **DEPRIVES** THE DEPARTED **SOUL** OF REST AND A PLACE IN THE HAPPY HUNTING GROUND, THE TWO TRIBES ARE LOCKED IN A POLICY OF **MUTUAL EXTERMINATION**, AS LONG AS **EITHER** DRAWS A BREATH OF LIFE!

QUANAH, AS A NOVICE AND AN OUTSIDER — WITH A FAMOUS DADDY — HAS EVEN MORE TO PROVE THAN THE OTHER YOUTHS.

ALSO, THE TAINT OF **WHITE BLOOD** FLOWS IN HIS VEINS, A RARITY THAT SINGLES HIM OUT FROM THE REST....

AND MAKES THE TASTE OF VICTORY TWICE AS SWEET!

FOR THE TONKAWAS, PINNED ON THE CANYON FLOOR, IT IS OVER IN A BRUTAL INSTANT...

GET LOUD TALKER'S BODY. HE WAS A FOOL, BUT NO USE IN SHAMING HIS FAMILY BY LEAVING IT TO THE WOLVES.

57

NOT BAD, SON, BUT YOU'VE GOT A LONG WAY TO GO BEFORE YOU'RE AS GOOD AS PETA NOCONA!

!

DID YOU **HEAR** WHAT HAPPENED WHEN OLD BEAR CAUGHT HIM AND WEAKEAH TOGETHER DOWN AT THE CREEK? TEE HEE

OLD BEAR'S HANDSOME DAUGHTER, **WEAKEAH**, BRAZENLY ADORES QUANAH, AND, AS SLIGHTLY OLDER GIRLS ARE PRONE TO DO, SHE MANAGES TO MAKE HIM AWARE OF HER CHARMS.

LIKE MOST COMANCHE MAIDENS, SHE'S NOT **SHY** ABOUT IT, BUT SHE STILL DOESN'T WANT EVERYBODY IN THE VILLAGE **KNOWING** WHAT GOES ON — ESPECIALLY HER **PARENTS**!

AWFUL **HOT** TODAY, ISN'T IT ??

HMMM

SPLASH
SPLASH

DAUGHTER, YOU COME OUTTA THERE AND BE QUICK ABOUT IT!

UH-OH.

NOT THAT OLD BEAR HAS ANYTHING AGAINST QUANAH **PERSONALLY**. HE JUST WANTS WEAKEAH TO BE MORE **DISCREET**.

WHAT'S A MATTER WITH YOU, CARRYING ON IN BROAD **DAYLIGHT**! WHY, THE WHOLE TRIBE IS TALKING ABOUT IT!

..AND HIM POOR AS A GROUND SQUIRREL!

OH PAPA, HE'LL AMOUNT TO SOMETHING! JUST YOU WAIT!!

YEAH, SURE.. AND MEANWHILE, YOUR OTHER SUITORS, MEN OF MEANS, ARE BEGINNING TO WONDER! WHY JUST YESTERDAY TENNAP'S FATHER THREATENED TO CALL THE WHOLE THING OFF!!

TENNAP?!? OH, FATHER, HOW COULD YOU?? YOU KNOW I CAN'T STAND THAT.. THAT— FROG!

FROG?? FROG, IS IT? THAT'S NO WAY TO TALK ABOUT YOUR FUTURE HUSBAND! WHY, HE'S A MAN OF UP AND COMING IMPORTANCE — AND, HIS FATHER IS LOADED!! NOW YOU LISTEN TO YOUR OL' DADDY, HEAR?

HUMPHF!

TENNAP IS A VAIN AND SURLY FELLOW, CURSED WITH THE POCK-MARKS OF A CHILDHOOD DISEASE, BUT HE IS THE SON OF A WEALTHY AND POWERFUL WARRIOR WHO SPARES NO EXPENSE ON BEHALF OF HIS PAMPERED OFFSPRING.

AH, TENNAP, YOU HANDSOME ROGUE, YOU! THE GREAT SPIRIT'S GIFT TO WOMEN.. SIGH

YESSIR, YOU'LL HAVE A HARD TIME FINDING A BETTER HUSBAND FOR THAT SKINNY LITTLE OL' GIRL THAN MY FINE TENNAP!

GRUNT...

QUANAH SEETHES IN SILENT RAGE AS HE WATCHES THE CERTAIN OUTCOME OF SUPERIOR BARGAINING POWER.

NOW, I WAS GONNA OFFER YOU 12 HORSES FOR HER, BUT I'VE BEEN HEARING SOME MIGHTY DISTRESSING RUMORS LATELY...

THAT NIGHT, AT THEIR TRYSTING PLACE, AN ANXIOUS QUANAH HEARS THE WORST.

TEN PONIES!? A FORTUNE! WE'VE GOT TO THINK OF SOMETHING...

QUANAH EXPLAINS THE PROBLEM TO HIS COMRADES.

WE'D LIKE TO HELP YOU OUT, BROTHER—BUT **TEN** PONIES?!?

I'M DESPERATE— LOAN ME YOUR HORSES, I'LL REPAY YOU SOON AS WE CAN GET A RAID TOGETHER AND CAPTURE MORE!

BUT THE WILY TENNAP, SUSPECTING THAT QUANAH WILL TRY SOMETHING, POSTS A FRIEND TO **SPY** ON THE MEETING.

CAPTURE MORE? HOW WE GONNA' DO THAT, WHEN WE'RE ALL ON **FOOT**??

NEVERTHELESS, QUANAH PERSUADES THEM. EARLY THE NEXT MORNING, ARRAYED IN HIS FINEST BUCKSKINS AND ORNAMENTS, HE PROUDLY LEADS TEN HORSES TO THE LODGE OF OLD BEAR.

TO HIS DISMAY, TENNAP IS THERE AS WELL, NOT WITH **TEN** BUT WITH **TWENTY** HORSES!

YOU'RE **TOO LATE,** LOVER BOY. OLD BEAR HAS ALREADY ACCEPTED MY BRIDAL PRICE! IN TWO MOONS, SHE WILL BELONG TO ME, AND ME ALONE! UNDERSTAND??

HA HA HA

I'VE GOT A PLAN.. BUT IF WE GET CAUGHT, THERE'LL BE BAD TROUBLE NOW, LISTEN—

SOB SOB

AFTER THE MOON SETS, A FIGURE SILENTLY GLIDES FROM OLD BEAR'S LODGE AND JOINS ANOTHER HIDDEN IN THE SHADOWS.

PSSST!

TOGETHER THEY CREEP TO THE EDGE OF THE SLEEPING CAMP, WHERE TWENTY-ONE YOUNG BRAVES AND A FEW BOLD MAIDENS AWAIT THEM WITH PROVISIONS AND EXTRA MOUNTS.

THEY MYSTERIOUSLY MAKE IT PAST THE NIGHT GUARD.

I CAN'T WAIT TO SEE THE LOOK ON OL' TENNAP'S FACE..

BOY, IS HE GONNA BE BENT OUT OF SHAPE!

AND SO BEGINS THE ELOPEMENT OF QUANAH AND WEAKEAH, ACCOMPANIED BY A BRAVE GROUP OF FRIENDS WHO CAST THEIR FATES IN WITH THE TWO LOVERS. WIFE STEALING IS NO SMALL THING TO THE COMANCHES — DISFIGUREMENT FOR THE WOMAN, DISHONOR FOR THE MAN — SOMETIMES EVEN *BANISHMENT*!

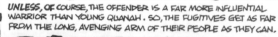

UNLESS, OF COURSE, THE OFFENDER IS A FAR MORE INFLUENTIAL WARRIOR THAN YOUNG QUANAH. SO, THE FUGITIVES GET AS FAR FROM THE LONG, AVENGING ARM OF THEIR PEOPLE AS THEY CAN.

TRAVELLING NIGHTS AND HIDING DAYS, THE EXILE BAND WORKS ITS WAY DEEP INTO TEXAS, NEAR THE CONCHOS. THERE THEY ESTABLISH A HIDDEN BASE FOR RAIDS ON THE HORSEHERDS OF OUTLYING SETTLERS AND STOCKMEN.

THEY HAVE SOON ACCUMULATED A CONSIDERABLE HERD.

NOT BAD FOR BEGINNERS..

MEANWHILE, TENNAP AND HIS FATHER ARE *FUMING*.

JUST WAIT TILL I FIND THAT SCOUNDREL. I'LL *WRING HIS NECK* WITH MY BARE HANDS!

LOOK, I FEEL BAD ABOUT THIS TOO, BUT IT'S NOT MY FAULT. A DEAL IS A DEAL, RIGHT ?? DON'T WORRY, SHE'LL TURN UP, SOONER OR LATER..

YOU HAVE **SHAMED ME,** QUANAH, BEFORE THE EYES OF OUR PEOPLE!!

IT WAS NOT MY INTENTION TO INJURE YOU, TENNAP. I ONLY TOOK WHAT WAS ALREADY MINE!

YOURS?!? WHAT OF MY BRIDAL PRICE!? TWENTY GOOD HORSES I PAID OLD BEAR FOR THAT **HUSSY,** AND HE WON'T GIVE THEM BACK!

I AM **RICH** IN HORSES NOW, AND I DO NOT WISH COMANCHE BLOOD TO BE SPILLED THIS DAY. YET.. WE WILL **FIGHT YOU** IF FIGHT WE MUST!!

TENNAP SCANS THE MENACING BRAVES OF QUANAH'S STRONGHOLD AND KNOWS THAT **MUCH BLOOD** WILL INDEED FLOW IF THERE IS FIGHTING — **HIS OWN BLOOD,** MOST CERTAINLY. HE SQUIRMS UNEASILY IN HIS SADDLE.

WAIT! WHAT'S AT STAKE HERE — HONOR, RIGHT? SO WHY DON'T WE SMOKE THE PIPE AND SEE IF HONOR CAN BE UPHELD...

OKAY, IT'S A DEAL...

YOU CAME OUT OF THAT SMELLING LIKE A ROSE TENNAP. THESE ARE MUCH BETTER HORSES THAN THE ONES YOU GAVE FOR HER!

YEAH, YOU'RE RIGHT. SHE WAS ONLY WORTH MAYBE TEN IN THE FIRST PLACE! MY DADDY IS GONNA BE TICKLED PINK!!

THEIR CONFLICT RESOLVED, QUANAH AND HIS FOLLOWERS RETURN TO THEIR BAND, BUT NOW THEY BRING **MANY HORSES** WITH THEM — AND MORE **PRESTIGE** THAN WHEN THEY LEFT. QUANAH'S STAR IS ON THE RISE AMONG THE QUOHADAS.

THAT'S QUANAH THERE.. MY, BUT HE'S A GOOD-LOOKING DEVIL! HE CAN CARRY ME OFF ANY TIME HE FEELS LIKE IT!

AND I HEARD THAT TENNAP HAD TO SETTLE FOR ONE LESS HORSE THAN HE GAVE HER FATHER.

WE WANTED YOU FOR OUR DAUGHTER ANYWAY, MY SON... BUT TIMES ARE HARD, AND TWENTY HORSES ARE TWENTY HORSES!

THE PAPER TALK

DURING THE EARLY YEARS OF THE **CIVIL WAR**, THE COMANCHES ARE CONFUSED BY THE NATURE OF THE WHITE-MAN'S STRUGGLE, BUT USUALLY WILLING TO SHOW UP WHEREVER PRESENTS ARE BEING HANDED OUT.

YEAH, THE PAPER SAYS YOU'RE A *HEAP GOOD FRIEND* OF *THE WHITE SOLDIERS*.. ONLY TROUBLE IS, IT'S SIGNED BY THE *BLUECOAT* CAPTAIN UP AT FORT GIBSON !!

OOPS..

THEY SOON FIND THAT THE MEN IN GREY PROMISE MORE THAN THEY CAN DELIVER.

I'M SORRY CHIEF, BUT... YOUR PRESENTS HAVE BEEN ..UH.. HELD UP BY A DOCK STRIKE IN NEW ORLEANS.

YEAH, THE YANKEES STRUCK IT !

THAT AND THEIR TRADITIONAL HATRED FOR THE *TEJANOS* EVENTUALLY SWAY THEM TO ALLIANCES WITH THE UNION, ESPECIALLY AS THEY LEARN OF THE TEXANS' INABILITY TO PROTECT THEIR EXPOSED NORTHERN FRONTIER.

THEY KNOW WE'RE LEAVING..

GOD HELP THE FOLKS WHO AIN'T !

UNDER MILITANT CHIEFS LIKE WILD HORSE, LITTLE BUFFALO, SANACO, HORSEBACK AND OTHERS, THE **COMANCHES** AND THEIR KIOWA ALLIES BECOME *BOLDER* IN ATTACKING THE SETTLEMENTS.

ALL THE SOLDIERS HAVE GONE TO FIGHT IN THE *BIG WAR* — NOW IS OUR CHANCE! WHO WILL RIDE WITH ME?

A NEW KIND OF RAID APPEARS AS THEY LEARN THAT THE UNION AGENTS WILL BUY STOLEN **CATTLE**.

QUANAH RIDES ON MANY OF THESE, LIKE THE RAID AT ELM CREEK, INCREASING HIS REPUTATION AS A FEARLESS SUBCHIEF.

BRING US ALL YOU CAN GET. WE'LL SEE HOW THOSE DAMN TEXANS LIKE EATING COLLARD GREENS INSTEAD OF STEAKS!

BUT IT IS NOT JUST SPOILS AND CATTLE THAT THE RAIDERS WANT. THEY WANT *REVENGE* FOR ALL THE WRONGS THEIR PEOPLE HAVE SUFFERED AT THE HANDS OF THE HATED *TEJANOS*.

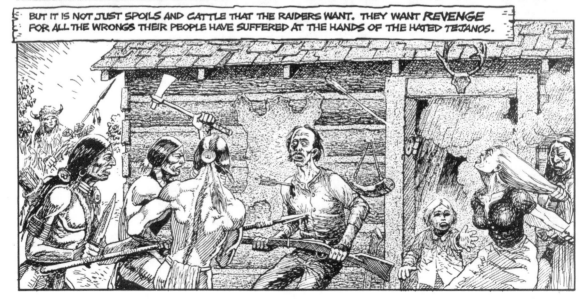

THE BORDERLANDS PRESENT A *PITIFUL SPECTACLE* — HOMES IN ASHES, FIELDS GROWN UP WITH WEEDS, LIVESTOCK RUNNING WILD ON THE OPEN RANGE — AS THEIR PLUNDERING REACHES HALFWAY ACROSS A TEXAS DRAINED OF ITS FIGHTING MEN BY THE DISTANT WAR.

THE FRONTIER REGIMENT, A MAKE-SHIFT GROUP OF VOLUNTEERS, IS ORGANIZED BY THE STATE TO PROTECT THE HOMEFRONT, BUT USUALLY IT IS A CASE OF "TOO LITTLE, TOO LATE".

THE NORTHERN FRONTIER IS DEPOPULATED AND PUSHED BACK A HUNDRED MILES AS THE INDIANS MAUL THE ISOLATED SETTLEMENTS. PETA NOCONA WOULD HAVE APPROVED...

67

AS THE CIVIL WAR ENDS AND THE SOLDIERS RETURN— BLUE INSTEAD OF GREY— SOME OF THE OLDER CHIEFS COUNSEL PEACE, UNTIL THEY CAN DETERMINE WHAT IT ALL MEANS.

BUT THIS SIMPLE FACT— THAT THE RETURNING REBS ARE A CONQUERED PEOPLE— ONLY MAKES THE YOUNG WAR-CHIEFS MORE DARING. THE RAIDING INCREASES.

THE BLUECOATS MAY LEAVE US ALONE. IT WAS OUR TEJANO ENEMIES WHO WORE GREY, AND THEY ARE BEATEN! I SAY, WAIT.

COULD IT BE THAT MANY WINTERS AND SITTING AT THE FEET OF THE WHITE FATHER HAVE COOLED THE FIGHTING ARDOR OF THE VENERABLE TEN BEARS? OUR ENEMIES CANNOT PURSUE US. THE BLUECOATS FORBID IT!! I SAY MORE TALK IS FOOLISH! LET US ACT!

YES   YES   YES

SOON THE TAKING AND HOLDING OF WHITE CAPTIVES FOR RANSOM BECOMES A BRISK AND LUCRATIVE INDIAN SIDELINE.

MORE FUN THAN STEALING COWS... AND A LOT MORE PROFITABLE!

ALTHO SOME OF THE LEADING OFFENDERS HAD BEEN SIGNERS OF A TREATY AT THE WAR'S END, AGENT FOR THE SOUTHERN TRIBES, COL. J.H. LEAVENWORTH, FEELS THAT **PEACE** CAN ACCOMPLISH MORE THAN WAR.

SATANTA SAY BECAUSE HE LIKE YOU SO MUCH, HE DO YOU A FAVOR— ONLY $100 FOR THIS ONE, PLUS MY USUAL...

THIS IS ROBBERY, YOU KNOW..

UNDAUNTED BY THE APPARENT FAILURE OF LEAVEN-WORTH'S POLICY, THE GREAT WHITE FATHER IN WASH-INGTON SPREADS THE WORD OF A BIG PEACE TALK, TO BE HELD ON THE BANKS OF MEDICINE LODGE CREEK.

Y'ALL COME, NOW.. THERE'S GONNA' BE COFFEE, BARBEQUE, AND WAGONLOADS OF GIFTS...

ALL THE TRIBES OF THE SOUTHERN PLAINS GATHER TO HEAR HIS WORDS — THE CHEYENNES, ARAPAHOES, KIOWAS, KIOWA-APACHES, AND THE WEAKER COMANCHE BANDS, LIKE THE PENATEKAS, YAMPARIKAS, AND NOCONIS.

WHEN DO WE GET THE PRESENTS?

MISSOURI SENATOR JOHN B. HENDERSON, SPOKESMAN FOR THE PEACE COMMISSION, OUTLINES THE GREAT FATHER'S WISHES.

ALL THESE *TERRIBLE* THINGS WE HEAR ABOUT YOU MAKE US FEEL SAD.. BUT WE'RE WILLING TO LISTEN TO YOUR SIDE. WHAT EXACTLY DO YOU PEOPLE WANT, ANYWAY?

REPRESENTING THE KIOWAS IS SATANTA, THE EPITOME OF THE UNTAMED SAVAGE.

THIS IS MY COUNTRY, AND I DON'T LIKE YOU COMING IN AND MESSING WITH IT! AS TO ALL THESE LITTLE HOUSES, FARMING, AND WELFARE LINES, YOU CAN FORGET ABOUT IT — WE DON'T WANT THEM! WHEN A KIOWA IS PENNED UP, HE GROWS WEAK AND DIES..

TEN BEARS, OLDER, WISER AND MORE CAUTIOUS THAN THE COCKY SATANTA, SPEAKS ELOQUENTLY FOR THE YAMPARIKAS.

IF THE TEXANS HAD KEPT OUT OF MY COUNTRY, THERE MIGHT HAVE BEEN PEACE. BUT IT IS TOO LATE. NOW THEY HAVE THE COUNTRY WHICH WE LOVED, AND WE WISH ONLY TO WANDER ON THE PRAIRIE UNTIL WE DIE...

I LOVE TO CARRY OUT THE TALK OF THE GREAT FATHER, BUT DO NOT ASK US TO GIVE UP THE FREE LIFE AND THE BUFFALO. IT MAKES THE YOUNG MEN SAD AND ANGRY. DO NOT SPEAK OF IT MORE!!

BUT IN THE END, TEN BEARS PUTS HIS MARK TO THE WHITEMAN'S PAPER, CEDING THE COMANCHE HEARTLAND AND PLEDGING RESERVATION LIFE FOR HIS PEOPLE. THE DEFIANT SATANTA, FOR ALL HIS BLUSTER, SIGNS AS WELL.

IT'S BEEN A REAL PLEASURE, CHIEF, BELIEVE ME...

IF YOU'RE EVER IN WASHINGTON, DON'T FORGET TO STOP IN AND SAY HI...

NOW YOU GET THE PRESENTS!

IT IS AT MEDICINE LODGE THAT QUANAH LEARNS OF HIS MOTHER'S CRUEL FATE.

SHE KEPT TRYING TO RUN AWAY.. FINALLY STARVED HERSELF TO DEATH AFTER THE LITTLE GIRL DIED OF FEVER...

THE HOSTILE QUOHADAS AND KOTSOTEKAS, ALOOF AS USUAL, ARE NOT PRESENT AT THE COUNCIL TALKS, BUT THEY FOLLOW ITS PROCEEDINGS CLOSELY...

WHAT ARE THEY GIVING AWAY NOW?

YOU WOULDN'T BELIEVE IT...

QUANAH **SCOFFS** AT THE OLD CHIEFS WHO SIGN THE TREATIES FOR HANDOUTS. TO HIM, THE TALKS INDICATE **WEAKNESS** ON THE PART OF THE WHITES.

WHY SHOULD WE ACCEPT THE WHITEMAN'S TRINKETS? WE CAN TAKE ALL WE WANT, ANYTIME, AS COMANCHES ALWAYS HAVE — WITH *THIS!!*

OTHER YOUNG LEADERS, LIKE **WHITE HORSE** OF THE KIOWAS, ALSO SHUN THE COUNCIL AND THROW THEIR LOT IN WITH THE UNBENDING QUOHADAS.

I'LL EAT BUFFALO CHIPS BEFORE I'D LIVE IN A HOUSE THAT YOU CAN'T **MOVE** WHEN THE TRASH PILES UP — WE'RE WITH *YOU*, QUANAH!

QUANAH REMEMBERS THE FATE OF HIS PENATEKA COUSINS IN TEXAS WHO TRUSTED THE PAPER TALK. HE LEADS HIS BAND AWAY FROM MEDICINE LODGE. WITHOUT HIM AND HIS WARRIORS, THE NEW "PEACE" TREATY IS MEANINGLESS.

TELL THE WHITE CHIEFS THAT THE *QUOHA-DAS* ARE **WARRIORS**, AND WILL LIVE ON A RESERVATION ONLY WHEN THE BLUECOATS COME AND *WHIP US*, OUT ON THE STAKED PLAINS!

QUANAH TAKES HIS BAND FAR AWAY FROM THE WHITEMEN AND THEIR PAPER PROMISES. THE QUOHADAS HUNT, MAKE WAR AND LIVE AS THEY ALWAYS HAVE. THE CONFUSING WORLD OF THE PALEFACES SEEMS DISTANT AND REMOTE, LIKE A FLEETING, BAD DREAM, WITHOUT SUBSTANCE, WITHOUT THREAT TO THE TIMELESS COMANCHE WAY OF LIFE.

LAST DAYS OF FREEDOM

IN KEEPING WITH HIS GROWING IMPORTANCE, HE ACQUIRES SEVERAL NEW WIVES.

72

THE INDIANS WHO STAY ON THE RESERVATION AROUND FT. SILL QUICKLY GROW DISILLUSIONED.

JUNK, THAT'S ALL IT IS...

HATS?

WHERE'S THE GUNS WE WERE SUPPOSED TO GET?

GUESS THEY EXPECT US TO HUNT WITH BUGLES!

UGH—CORN HURTS MY TEETH!!

GIVE IT TO THE HORSES..MAYBE THEY CAN EAT IT.

MANY DRIFT BACK TO THEIR BISON RANGES TO HUNT—AND TO RAID!

LET'S GO FIND QUANAH AND THE QUOHADAS TILL NEXT PAYDAY..

ONCE OUT ON THE PLAINS, THE ANGRY TRIBES—PARTICULARLY THE KIOWAS—TALK OF OPEN WAR.

I SAY WE'VE BEEN CLEANED OUT! WE OUGHT TO FIGHT!!

BUT QUANAH, HIGH ON THE STAKED PLAINS, HAS NEVER STOPPED FIGHTING. HE CONTINUES TO RAID INTO MEXICO AND DRIVE OFF TEXAS STOCK.

IF WE'RE NOT CAREFUL, THERE WON'T BE ANYONE **LEFT** TO RAISE CATTLE FOR US TO STEAL..

THE THIN STRING OF FORTS THROUGH-OUT WEST TEXAS IS UNABLE TO CONTAIN THE FAST-MOVING MARAUDERS AS THEY STORM FORTH FROM THE SAFETY OF THEIR RESERVATION TO PLUNDER THE FRONTIER. COMANCHERO TRADERS FROM NEW MEXICO RENDEZVOUS WITH THE RETURNING RAIDERS TO EXCHANGE NEEDED SUPPLIES FOR THEIR BOOTY.

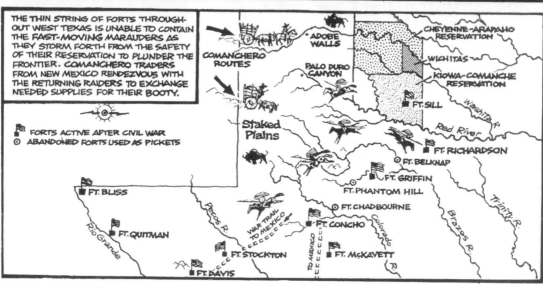

🚩 FORTS ACTIVE AFTER CIVIL WAR
⊙ ABANDONED FORTS USED AS PICKETS

COMANCHERO ROUTES

ADOBE WALLS

PALO DURO CANYON

Staked Plains

CHEYENNE-ARAPAHO RESERVATION

WICHITAS

KIOWA-COMANCHE RESERVATION

FT. SILL

Washita R.

Red River

FT. RICHARDSON

FT. BELKNAP

FT. GRIFFIN

FT. PHANTOM HILL

FT. CHADBOURNE

FT. BLISS

Pecos R.

FT. QUITMAN

Rio Grande

WAR TRAIL TO MEXICO

FT. CONCHO

FT. STOCKTON

TO MEXICO

FT. McKAVETT

Colorado R.

Brazos R.

Trinity R.

FT. DAVIS

BUILT AND MANNED BY UNTRIED BLACK TROOPS, MANY OF WHICH ARE ILLITERATE EX-SLAVES, THE NEW LINE OF DEFENSE IS A HIGHLY CONTROVERSIAL EXPERIMENT IN ESTABLISHED MILITARY CIRCLES.

YOU MEN HURRY IT UP OVER THERE! I GOT YOU ON WOOD CHOPPIN' DETAIL!

JOIN TH' ARMY AND LEARN A TRADE, TH' MAN SAID..

SOME TRADE!

THE BLACK CAVALRYMEN, "BUFFALO SOLDIERS" AS THE REDMEN TERM THEM, ARE SUBJECTED TO A ROUTINE OF ENDLESS, FRUSTRATING PATROL DUTY OVER THE TRACKLESS PLAINS, THEIR PREY AS ELUSIVE AS THE WIND.

LORD, WHAT AM I DOING HERE!?..

NOT ONLY ARE THEY EXPECTED TO DEFEND THE FAR-FLUNG FRONTIER FROM INDIAN DEPREDATIONS, CATTLE RUSTLING, AND STAGECOACH ROBBERY, BUT SOMETIMES THEY MUST DEFEND THEMSELVES FROM THE VERY PEOPLE THEY ARE MEANT TO PROTECT — THE EMBITTERED WHITE CITIZENS UNDER THE YOKE OF RECONSTRUCTION !!

HEY BOAH, WHERE'D YOU GIT THAT FANCY YANKEE UNIFORM??

DON'T PAY NO MIND, LEROY..

BLACK TROOPERS OF THE NINTH AND TENTH OFTEN HAVE TO MAKE DO WITH SUBSTANDARD OR USED EQUIPMENT AND MOUNTS, CAST OFF FROM THE MORE GLAMOROUS UNITS LIKE CUSTER'S SEVENTH CAVALRY.

WELL.. HERE'S TH' HORSES WE'VE BEEN WAITING MONTHS FOR..

THEY LOOK GOOD COMPARED TO TH' LAST BUNCH!

WHEEZE

75

OVER THE COMANCHEROS' DEEP-RUTTED TRAILS, QUANAH GETS ALL THE ARMS AND AMMUNITION HE NEEDS.

THROUGH THE ILLICIT COMANCHERO TRADE, NEW MEXICO IS RAPIDLY FILLING UP WITH STOLEN TEXAS CATTLE.

GOT SOME MORE COWS FOR YOU, JOSE?..

BUENO! TAKE A LOOK AT THESE, QUANAH. REPEATERS! BETTER THAN THE SOLDIERS GOT!! AND PISTOLS, TOO..

IN THE FACE OF INCREASED RAIDING AND THEIR HELPLESS-NESS IN DEALING WITH IT, THE MILITARY MEN AT FT. SILL BEGIN TO CHAFE AT THE GOVERNMENT'S PEACE POLICY.

WE'RE FEEDING, CLOTHING, AND ARMING THESE RASCALS AND THEN THEY'RE SLIPPING OFF THE RESERVATION, RAIDING IN TEXAS, AND EXPECTING US TO BUY BACK THEIR CAPTIVES! IT'S GOT TO STOP!

EVEN THE PERSEVERING AGENT, LAWRIE TATUM, BEGINS TO DOUBT THE WISDOM OF HIS MISSION.

COULD IT BE THAT MY RED CHILDREN ARE DECEIVING ME?

FINALLY THE PUBLIC FUROR BRINGS SHERMAN, COMMANDER OF THE ARMY, TO PERSONALLY ASSESS THE FRONTIER SITUATION.

SHERMAN IS SKEPTICAL OF THE SETTLERS' CLAIMS. HE TRAVELS THROUGH HOSTILE TERRITORY WITH A LIGHT ESCORT.

LITTLE DOES THE FAMED GENERAL SUSPECT THAT— BUT FOR A QUIRK OF KIOWA MEDICINE — HE WOULD NEVER HAVE REACHED HIS DESTINATION.

WHILE AT FT. RICHARDSON, SHERMAN IS PRESENTED WITH EVIDENCE HE CANNOT IGNORE — THE MASSACRE OF A TEAMSTER TRAIN ON THE VERY ROAD HE HAD TRAVELLED ONLY HOURS BEFORE.

A SCOUTING PARTY HASTENS TO SALT CREEK PRAIRIE FOR CONFIRMATION OF ONE OF THE WOUNDED SURVIVOR'S GRUESOME TALE.

NOT A PRETTY SIGHT..

NAW-SIR, IT SURE AIN'T.

THREE KIOWA CHIEFS ARE ARRESTED FOR OPENLY ADMITTING TO THE GRISLY WARREN WAGONTRAIN RAID.

ME AND MY BIG MOUTH!

IT'S THE END OF THE ROPE FOR YOU GUYS.

(SATANTA, SATANK, AND BIG TREE WERE ARRESTED ON THE FRONT PORCH OF COL. GRIERSON'S QUARTERS AT FT. SILL.)

78

AS THEY ARE BEING SENT BACK TO TEXAS TO STAND TRIAL FOR MURDER, OLD SATANK STRIPS THE MANACLES FROM HIS WRISTS AND STABS A GUARD, ALL THE WHILE, SINGING THE DEATH CHANT OF THE KIOWA WARRIOR ELITE.

OH SUN, YOU REMAIN FOREVER, OH EARTH, YOU REMAIN FOREVER—

BEFORE SATANK CAN FREE THE GUARD'S JAMMED SPENCER CARBINE, HE IS QUICKLY SHOT DOWN...

BUT WE KOITSENKGA MUST DIE....

FIRE!

AND HIS BODY UNCEREMONIOUSLY DUMPED BESIDE THE ROAD.

MOVE IT OUT!

ALTHO SATANTA PLEADS HIS INNOCENCE, A GRIM JURY RETURNS A QUICK AND CERTAIN VERDICT— GUILTY!

IT'S THOSE OTHER, BAD INDIANS WHO GET ME IN TROUBLE. TURN ME LOOSE, AND I'LL BE GOOD.

THROUGH THE AGITATION OF HIGH PLACED GOVERNMENT OFFICALS, WHO FEAR THE HANGING OF SATANTA AND BIG TREE WOULD TRIGGER A FULL-SCALE PLAINS WAR, GOVERNOR DAVIS OF TEXAS RELUCTANTLY AGREES TO COMMUTE THEIR DEATH SENTENCES TO LIFE IMPRISONMENT IN HUNTSVILLE, A FATE WORSE THAN DEATH FOR THE TWO CHIEFS.

HEY CHIEF! WHAT'S THE MATTER— NO LIKEE MAKEE CHAIRS ?? HAHAHAHA

I'LL GO NUTS IF I DON'T GET OUTTA HERE..

IN THE AFTERMATH OF THE KIOWA RAIDS, SHERMAN DECIDES TO GET TOUGH. HE COMMISSIONS YOUNG COLONEL RANALD MACKENZIE AND THE FOURTH CAVALRY TO PUNISH AND ROUND UP THE HOSTILE BANDS THAT REMAIN OFF THE RESERVATION.

IF YOU CAN'T BRING THEM IN ALIVE, LEAVE THEM OUT THERE DEAD!

MACKENZIE SEARCHES DEEP INTO COMANCHE TERRITORY FOR SIGNS OF THE QUOHADAS.

QUANAH LEADS A DARING NIGHT CHARGE INTO THE SOLDIERS' CAMP, STAMPEDING AWAY OVER SIXTY OF THEIR HORSES AND PACK MULES — INCLUDING MACKENZIE'S FAVORITE PACER.

MACKENZIE, AT LAST ON THE TRAIL OF A COMANCHE VILLAGE, LEADS HIS SLEEPLESS, UNNERVED TROOPERS FORWARD. QUANAH'S WARRIORS, STRENGTHENED BY THOSE OF BULL BEAR, HARRASS HIM EVERY STEP OF THE WAY.

WOAH, WHOAH!

DAMMIT, THEY WON'T STAND STILL!

A BLUE NORTHER AND FREEZING RAINS FURTHER HAMPER THE SOLDIERS, WHO BROUGHT NO HEAVY WINTER GEAR.

AT THIS RATE, THE HORSES WON'T LAST LONG..

AND THEN, NEITHER WILL WE..

FIZZ

CAUGHT OUT ON THE NAKED STAKED PLAINS IN SUB-ZERO WEATHER, MACKENZIE IS FORCED TO ABANDON THE CHASE.

WE WERE CLOSE TO CATCHING THEM, BY THE LOOKS OF IT...

CLOSE DON'T COUNT..

BUT QUANAH BACKTRACKS AND CONTINUES TO DOG THE RETREATING COLUMN, WOUNDING MACKENZIE IN THE LEG.

LEMME GO! I'M ALRIGHT, I TELL YOU.

LIKE HELL YOU ARE!

CAN'T FIGURE OUT IF WE'RE THE HUNTERS OR THE HUNTED!

QUANAH HAS OUTFOXED MACKENZIE FOR NOW, BUT HE KNOWS THE STRUGGLE IS FAR FROM OVER.

THEY'LL BE BACK.

THE FOLLOWING SPRING, MACKENZIE — HIS LEG HEALED AND WISER IN THE WAYS OF GUERILLA WARFARE — PREPARES ANOTHER EXPEDITION.

WE'LL GET 'UM THIS TIME..

DURING THE HOT SUMMER MONTHS, HE PROBES THE VAST STAKED PLAINS, A FORBIDDING NO-MAN'S LAND, LOCATING PRECIOUS WATERHOLES, DISRUPTING THE COMANCHERO TRADE, AND GAINING INFORMATION FOR FUTURE CAMPAIGNS.

THIS IS GETTING TO BE A RISKY BUSINESS!

THINK I'LL GO BACK TO NEW MEX-ICO AND HERD SHEEP..

IN SEPTEMBER OF 1872 HE FINDS MOW-WAY'S VILLAGE ON THE RED RIVER, KILLING, BURNING, AND TAKING CAPTIVES.

THAT SAME NIGHT, QUANAH'S RAIDERS SWOOP DOWN AND *RETAKE* MOW-WAY'S CAPTURED HERD OF 3000 HORSES...

AFTER THIS, WE'LL *SHOOT* EVERY HORSE WE TAKE.

THE FACT THAT THEIR WOMEN AND CHILDREN ARE HELD BY THE WHITE WARRIORS HAS A SOBERING AFFECT ON THE HOSTILE LEADERS LIKE MOW-WAY AND BULL BEAR.

ANYBODY THAT PULLS ANY STUNTS WHILE *MY* WIVES AND KIDS ARE LOCKED UP, WILL HAVE TO ANSWER TO ME!

AND TO ME!

THROUGH THE INTERCESSION OF SEVERAL "PEACEFUL" CHIEFS, MANY PRISONER SWAPS ARE CONDUCTED THAT WINTER. THERE IS A BRIEF LULL IN THE FIGHTING.

SEE? THE WHITES AREN'T SO BAD. I GOT MY MOTHER-IN-LAW BACK, FAT AS EVER!

BY THE FOLLOWING SUMMER THE COMANCHES ARE SO PEACEFUL THAT ALL THE REMAINING INDIAN CAPTIVES ARE RELEASED TO THEIR JOYOUS FAMILIES, MUCH TO THE CHAGRIN OF THE KIOWAS, WHOSE TWO CHIEFS ARE STILL PRISONERS.

BULL BEAR THANKS THREE-FINGERS 'KENZIE. YOU HEAP GOOD PONY SOLDIER — LIKE COMANCHE!

JUST REMEMBER— THE FIRST TIME YOU MESS UP, IT'S BACK TO THE JOINT!

NOW, NOW, GOVERNOR, NO CALL FOR THREATS. I'M SURE THESE MEN HAVE LEARNED THEIR LESSON AND WILL GIVE US NO FURTHER TROUBLE.

A DISGUSTED SHERMAN WRITES DAVIS ABOUT WHAT HE THINKS OF THE GOVERNOR'S ACTION.

...our dr[?]... scout, I ran the risk of my life; and I said what I now say to you, that I will not again volunta[rily] assume that risk in the interest [of] your frontier.

I believe Satanta and Big Tree w[ill have] their revenge, if they have not alre[ady] had it, and if they are to have som[e] scalps, that yours is the first [to] be taken.

W.T. Sherma[n]

ALTHO QUANAH AND HIS PEOPLE ARE TIRED OF FIGHTING, REPORTS FROM THE RESERVATION CONVINCE HIM HE MUST RESIST TO THE END.

IT'S BAD OVER THERE. SOLDIERS BOSS US AROUND, RATIONS DON'T COME.. THE PEOPLE ARE COLD, SICK, HUNGRY.. THE CHILDREN GROW WEAK AND DIE..

WHAT REALLY CONCERNS THE YOUNG LEADER IS THE RAPIDLY DIMINISHING BUFFALO HERDS...

THE BUFFALO WAR

AT THIS RATE, WE'LL SOON STARVE ANYWAY...

84

PROFESSIONAL BUFFALO HUNTERS, ARMED WITH HIGH-POWERED RIFLES AND HAVING ALREADY WIPED OUT THE KANSAS HERDS, ARE INVADING THE SOUTHERN PLAINS BISON RANGE IN EVER INCREASING NUMBERS.

IT'S NASTY BUSINESS, BUT I HATE FARMING..

HIGH IN THE PANHANDLE, NEAR BENT'S OLD TRADING POST OF ADOBE WALLS, THE HUNTERS HAVE ENTRENCHED THEMSELVES.

3 BUCKS A HIDE ADDS UP FAST!

THE ARMY WINKS AT THEIR OPERATIONS, TECHNICALLY IN VIOLATION OF THE 1867 MEDICINE LODGE TREATY. SOME, LIKE GEN. SHERIDAN, OPENLY SUPPORT THE SLAUGHTER.

THESE HUNTERS HAVE DONE MORE IN THE LAST 2 YEARS TO SETTLE THE VEXED INDIAN QUESTION THAN THE ENTIRE ARMY HAS DONE IN THIRTY YEARS! LET THEM KILL, SKIN, AND SELL UNTIL THE BUFFALOES ARE EXTERMINATED, FOR ONLY THEN WILL WE ADVANCE CIVILIZATION, AND HAVE A LASTING PEACE!

TO ADD TO THE INDIANS' DISCONTENT, A RAIDING PARTY RETURNING FROM MEXICO IS CAUGHT TWICE BY SOLDIERS IN TEXAS AND DEALT SEVERE BLOWS ON BOTH OCCASIONS.

POUR IT ON 'UM!

AMONG THE TWENTY CASUALTIES ARE TAU-ANKIA, FAVORITE SON OF THE KIOWA CHIEF LONE WOLF, AND HIS COUSIN GUITAN — BOTH MEMBERS OF THE ARISTOCRATIC ONDE WARRIOR SOCIETY AND THE FLOWER OF KIOWA MANHOOD.

TAKE THE HORSES AND MAKE A BREAK FOR IT! WE'LL TRY TO HOLD THEM OFF..

WHEN NEWS OF THE DISASTER REACHES THE KIOWA CAMPS THERE IS A FRENZY OF GRIEF. THE BEREAVED LONE WOLF CUTS HIS HAIR, MUTILATES HIMSELF, KILLS HIS HORSES, AND BURNS HIS POSSESSIONS, VOWING REVENGE AGAINST TEXANS.

BUT HIS EFFORT TO RETRIEVE THE BONES OF HIS BELOVED SON IS FRUSTRATED BY THE CLOSING RING OF TROOPERS.

THE SPRING OF 1874 FINDS THE INDIANS IN AN UGLY MOOD AS THEY SUDDENLY REALIZE THAT THEIR OLD WAY OF LIFE IS SLIPPING AWAY FOREVER.

WHAT BUSINESS DO THE BLUECOATS HAVE, MESSING IN OUR MEXICAN WAR?? I TELL YOU, THINGS ARE PRETTY BAD OFF WHEN A MAN CAN'T EVEN MAKE A DECENT LIVING!!

GRUNT

GRUNT!

GRUNT!

NOT KNOWING WHICH WAY TO TURN, SUDDENLY IN THEIR MIDST APPEARS A PROPHET, A QUOHADA MYSTIC NAMED ISATAI — "COYOTE SHIT"—AND HE TELLS THE CONFUSED TRIBES WHAT TO DO.

LOOK AT THE TRIBES THAT HAVE WALKED THE PEACE PATH — THE CADDOS, THE WICHITAS! ONCE THEY WERE MIGHTY WARRIORS, THEIR WIVES AND CHILDREN FAT, BUT NOW THEY ARE LEAN AND HUNGRY! THEY ARE GOING DOWN FAST.

THEY CAN'T EVEN DRESS THEMSELVES WITHOUT RUNNING TO THE WHITEMAN FOR HELP!

THERE'S ONLY ONE THING THAT WILL GUARANTEE THE STRENGTH OF OUR PEOPLE AND THE RETURN OF THE GOOD TIMES — DEATH TO ALL WHITES!! WE MUST DRIVE THEM ALL FROM THE LAND!!

AMONG THE MOST FERVENT OF ISATAI'S FOLLOWERS IS THE SUB-CHIEF QUANAH, FOR THE MESSIAH'S THOUGHTS ECHO HIS OWN.

DEATH!

DEATH!!

DEATH!!!

THOUGH HE IS SELF-PROCLAIMED AND AN UNTRIED WARRIOR, ISATAI BURNS WITH A VISION, AND HIS ZEAL IS CONTAGIOUS.

SPREAD THE WORD — WE'LL HAVE A SUN DANCE AND MAKE POWERFUL WAR MEDICINE. THE GREAT SPIRIT WILL SPEAK TO US IN PERSON.. I, ISATAI, PROMISE IT!!

THUS QUANAH BECOMES A MAJOR BOOSTER OF ISATAI'S CAUSE. HE WORKS TIRELESSLY TO RECRUIT ADHERENTS FOR THE HOLY WAR, EVEN AMONG THE PESSIMISTIC OLDER CHIEFS.

YOU'RE A PRETTY GOOD FIGHTER, QUANAH, BUT YOU DON'T KNOW EVERYTHING...

TAKE THE PIPE FIRST AGAINST THE BUFFALO HUNTERS. IF YOU CAN KILL THEM, COME BACK AND THEN WE'LL TALK ABOUT A BIG WAR!

SO, IN AN EFFORT TO UNITE ALL THE SOUTHERN PLAINS TRIBES IN A WAR TO SAVE THE BUFFALO, THE COMANCHES CONVERGE ON ELM CREEK FOR THEIR FIRST ATTEMPT AT A SUN DANCE CEREMONY.

AN ELABORATE LODGE IS CONSTRUCTED TO HOUSE THE PROCEEDINGS AS THE VARIOUS TRIBES CONTINUE TO GATHER.

THE KIOWAS ARE REPRESENTED BY ONLY A FEW CHIEFS, BUT ALL OF THEM MEN OF NOTED WORTH — LIKE THE GRIEVING LONE WOLF, WHOSE SON'S BONES STILL LIE IN TEXAS, WHITE HORSE, WOMAN'S HEART, WHITE SHIELD, HOWLING WOLF, AND BIG BOW. THEY LISTEN EAGERLY TO THE WAR TALK, FOR THEIR ATTEMPT AT RESERVATION LIFE HAS BEEN HARD, AND THEY LONG FOR THE DAYS WHEN THEY WERE MASTERS. EVEN SATANTA, RISKING HIS PAROLE, IS THERE TO WITNESS THE AFFAIR.

..AND IF WE DON'T DO SOMETHING FAST, THE HERDS WILL ALL BE GONE!

FROM THE NORTH COME SPLINTER GROUPS OF ARAPAHOS AND CHEYENNE DOG SOLDIERS, WELL ARMED AND IN A FIGHTING MOOD.

WE'RE SICK OF THE OLD MEN'S WAY. WE BRING 80 NEW WINCHESTERS TO USE AGAINST THE WHITES.

EVEN THE PENATEKAS, NOCONIS, AND YAMPARIKAS, LONG AC-CUSTOMED TO RESERVATION LIFE, ARE REPRESENTED, ALTHO THEY GROW NERVOUS AT THE TALK OF OUTRIGHT WAR.

FIRST, WE AVENGE LONE WOLF'S KINFOLKS, THEN WE GET RID OF THOSE ACCURSED TONKAWA SCOUTS AND WHITE BUFFALO HUNTERS!!

THEY'VE GONE LOCO...

SEE? I TOLD YOU IT'D BE LIKE THIS!

BUT THE DOMINANT VOICES IN THE WAR FACTION ARE THE QUOHADAS AND KOTSOTEKAS, AND QUANAH IS THEIR SPOKESMAN.

IT IS TRUE THAT LONE WOLF'S KINS-MEN MUST BE AVENGED. I, TOO, HAVE A BLOOD DEBT TO SETTLE WITH THE TONKAWAS. BUT IT IS THE *HIDE HUNTERS* THAT WE SHOULD STRIKE *FIRST!* THE PLAINS MUST BE CLEANSED OF THEIR STENCH!

HOW WE GONNA' DO ALL THAT?? WE'RE LOW ON AMMO...

DON'T WORRY, COYOTE SHIT HERE, CAN VOMIT WAGONLOADS OF THE STUFF..

HOW DO WE KNOW HE'S NOT PUTTING US ON?

NOT ONLY THAT, BUT I CAN STOP THEIR BULLETS IN MID-AIR, JUST BY A FLICK OF THE WRIST!

YEAH, HOW?

GOSH..

WHAT!?! DOUBTERS?? DIDN'T YOU SEE THE GREAT FIRE-TAILED STAR THAT LIT THE SKY FOR 5 DAYS LAST YEAR? I FORETOLD ITS COMING, YOU KNOW...

HE'S RIGHT— WE ALL SAW IT... HIS MEDICINE IS VERY STRONG!

I EVEN SAW HIM RAISE THE DEAD!!

THEN IT'S SETTLED!!! DANCE, SUMMONS THE GREAT SPIRIT, AND WE'LL BE INVULNERABLE! TO CINCH IT, I'LL EVEN MIX UP SOME PAINT FOR YOU THAT WILL MELT BULLETS BEFORE THEY STRIKE!

IN THE DAYS THAT FOLLOW, THE WILD BANDS DANCE UNTIL THEIR SPIRITS MERGE. CHEAP WHISKEY, OBTAINED FROM THE COMANCHEROS, BOLSTERS THEIR RESOLVE, IF NOT THEIR AGREEMENT ON DETAILS.

HUH-YUH-EE

ELE-YUH-AHH-HUH-YU

I SAY THASH... HIC... TH' WAY TO DO IT !!..

NAW, YOU'RE ALL WET...WE GOTTA BLA BLA

SOME OF THE TIMID CHIEFS, GREY LEGGINGS, MILKY WAY, AND OTHERS, REFUSE THE WARPIPE AND HURRY OFF TO THE AGENCY SO THEY WON'T BE INVOLVED IN THE INEVITABLE BLOODSHED.

EVEN SATANTA, ONCE THE FIERCEST WARRIOR OF THEM ALL, DECLINES TO RIDE THE WAR TRAIL. PRISON HAS MADE HIM A CHANGED MAN.

COME BACK HERE, YOU COWARDS!

STAND UP AND BE A MAN!

THOSE HOTHEADS ARE GOING TO GET US ALL IN TROUBLE.

C'MON, WHITE BEAR, YOU'RE GONNA MISS OUT ON ALL TH' FUN!

SORRY FELLERS, I'D LIKE TO GO, BUT I CAN'T TAKE A CHANCE ON GETTING THROWN BACK IN TH' POKEY.

AT LAST THE WARPARTY, ONE OF THE LARGEST EVER FIELDED ON THE SOUTHERN PLAINS, RIDES AGAINST ITS FIRST OBJECTIVE — THE HIDE HUNTERS AT ADOBE WALLS !!

FORTIFIED BY COMANCHERO WHISKEY AND THE INFLAMMATORY ORATION OF ISATAI, THE WARRIORS DON THEIR MAGIC SHIRTS AND WARPAINT, AND PREPARE FOR A DAWN ATTACK ON THE ENCAMPMENT.

91

QUANAH'S BRAVES CHARGE THE CITADEL TIME AFTER TIME, FALLING UNDER WITHERING FIRE FROM INSIDE THE WALLS.

THE QUOHADA LEADER HAS A HORSE SHOT FROM UNDERNEATH HIM AND HAS TO SCRAMBLE FOR COVER BEHIND A ROTTING BUFFALO CARCASS.

HE IS RECOVERED, BADLY SHAKEN, BY A DARING WARRIOR.

ISATAI, VIEWING THE BATTLE FROM AFAR, RESPLENDENT IN HIS YELLOW MEDICINE PAINT, IS CONFRONTED BY A SWARM OF ANGRY CHEYENNES.

WHERE'S YOUR MAGIC NOW, WISEGUY? I OUGHT TO BUST YOUR HEAD!

HIM! IT'S HIS FAULT!

IF YOU'RE SO BULLET-PROOF, WHY DON'T YOU GO DOWN THERE AND GET MY SON'S BODY?!!

AT THAT VERY MOMENT, YOUNG BILLY DIXON, THE HUNTER WHO HAD SOUNDED THE ALARM, DRAWS A BEAD ON THE DISTANT GROUP.

BAT, SEE THEM INJUNS SITTIN' OVER YONDER?

GOOD GOD, BILLY— THAT MUST BE ALMOST A MILE AWAY!

THE BALL FROM HIS .50 CALIBER SHARPS KNOCKS ONE OF THE CHEYENNES OFF HIS HORSE JUST AS THE EN-RAGED WARRIOR IS ABOUT TO QUIRT THEIR FALSE PROPHET.

UUUUUHH...

THE FRAGILE ALLIANCE CRACKS AT DIXON'S IMPOSSIBLE SHOT.

GUNS SHOOT TO-
DAY, MAYBE SO KILL
YOU TOMORROW!

THIS IS BAD
MEDICINE — WE
BETTER CLEAR OUT
OF HERE..

QUANAH SEES HIS WARRIORS MELT SULLENLY AWAY FROM THE HUNTERS' STRONG-
HOLD, THEIR RESOLVE BROKEN BY THE FAILURE OF "COYOTE SHIT'S" MEDICINE.

NO USE TO
FIGHT ADOBE!

IT'S HOPELESS,
QUANAH — WE'VE AL-
READY LOST TOO
MANY MEN..

WE SHOULDN'T
HAVE GOTTEN MIXED
UP IN THIS..

IT'S NOT
OUR
QUARREL.

NEVER ARE THEY TO BE FIRMLY UNITED AGAIN, AND NEVER AGAIN DOES QUANAH TRUST A MEDICINE MAN.

SHUT UP— OR
ANOTHER SKUNK
WILL DIE!

IT'S NOT MY FAULT..
IF THOSE CHEYENNES
HADN'T KILLED THAT
SKUNK YESTERDAY,
EVERYTHING WOULD
BE OKAY.....

ALTHO QUANAH'S GRAND ALLIANCE IS SMASHED, SMALL WARPARTIES CONTINUE TO VENT THEIR WRATH ON LONE HUNTERS, TRAVELLERS, AND ISOLATED SETTLERS.

AS THE ATROCITIES GAIN IN NUMBER, THE PUBLIC OUTCRY BRINGS MACKENZIE AND HIS BATTLE-TOUGHENED TROOPERS BACK INTO THE FIELD. THE PEOPLE — AND THE ARMY — HAVE HAD A BELLYFUL OF THE "PEACE POLICY."

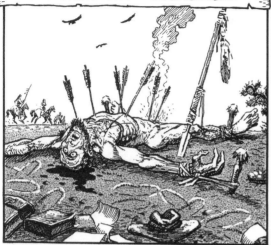

WRINKLED·HAND CHASE

BUT THIS TIME IT IS A MASSIVE, 5-PRONGED CAMPAIGN, DESIGNED TO CRIPPLE THE HOSTILES ONCE AND FOR ALL.

AT FIRST MACKENZIE HAS TROUBLE LOCATING HIS PREY.

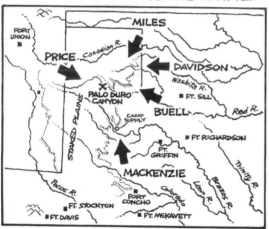

SEEMS LIKE I'VE BEEN THROUGH THIS BEFORE.

HEAVY RAINS MIRE THE ESSENTIAL SUPPLY WAGONS AND HAMPER THE MOVEMENTS OF HIS SOUTHERN COLUMN.

NOW DEEP INTO ENEMY TERRITORY, MACKENZIE TRIES TO AVOID THE COSTLY MISTAKES OF PAST CAMPAIGNS.

NO FIRES, KEEP YOUR BOOTS ON, WEAPONS READY, AND YOUR HORSES STAKED DOWN REAL GOOD!

SKIRMISHES BECOME FREQUENT AND THE COMMANDER'S HARD-LEARNED LESSONS PAY OFF. STILL, HE CAN FIND NO TARGET AGAINST WHICH TO DIRECT A DECISIVE BLOW.

HIYII EEHAAA

AS LUCK WOULD HAVE IT, HIS SEMINOLE-NEGRO SCOUTS CAPTURE A RENEGADE COMANCHERO, ON HIS WAY BACK FROM A RENDEZVOUS WITH THE INDIANS.

WHERE'S QUANAH AT, JOSE?

SENOR, I DON'T KNOW NO QUANAH..

THE NO-NONSENSE MACKENZIE HAS THE CAPTIVE'S NECK STRETCHED FROM A PROPPED-UP WAGONTREE.

I'LL ASK YOU ONE MORE TIME — WHERE ARE THE QUOHADAS HOLED UP?

GASP!..P-P.. CHOKE — PA.. PALO DURO!

SCOUTS ARE SENT 25 MILES AHEAD OF THE COLUMN WITH THE UNFORTUNATE JOSE TAFOYA. AS THEY PEER INTO THE MISTS OF THE YAWNING CANYON, HIS STORY IS CONFIRMED BY A VISTA OF TEEPEES AS FAR AS THE EYE CAN SEE.

IT'S THEM, ALRIGHT...

QUANAH'LL HAVE MY SKIN FOR THIS !!

CLOSE TO THE KILL AT LAST, MACKENZIE LEAVES HIS CUMBERSOME SUPPLY WAGONS UNDER GUARD AND FORCE-MARCHES HIS MEN THROUGH THE NIGHT.

IN THE GREY DAWN LIGHT, HE ISSUES RAPID ORDERS.

MR. THOMPSON, TAKE YOUR MEN DOWN AND RUN OFF THEIR HORSES. WE'LL BE RIGHT BEHIND YOU!!

YES SIR!

THE ONLY TRAIL DESCENDING TO THE CANYON FLOOR IS NARROW AND TREACHEROUS.

BUT THE VANGUARD MANAGES TO REACH THE BOTTOM AND MOUNT BEFORE THE SLEEPING VILLAGE COMES TO LIFE.

A AND E COMPANIES MAKE A RUSH TOWARD THE LODGES, BUT THE INDIANS — AROUSED BY NOW — FIGHT VALIANTLY, GIVING THEIR WOMEN AND CHILDREN TIME TO ESCAPE AMIDST A SCENE OF PANIC AND BEDLAM.

IN THEIR HASTE TO EVACUATE, THEY ARE FORCED TO ABANDON THEIR HORSEHERD TO THE ONSLAUGHT OF THE SOLDIERS.

BY THE TIME MACKENZIE HAS ENOUGH MEN ARRAYED TO ATTACK THE DEFENDERS IN THE ROCKS, THEY TOO HAVE MELTED INTO THE PLAINS ABOVE.

CAPTAIN GUNTHER, PULL YOUR MEN OFF THOSE ROCKS! THEY'LL NEVER REACH THE TOP ALIVE!!

HIS MEN EXHAUSTED, HE IS CONTENT TO LET THEM GO.

THE ABANDONED VILLAGES ARE EXAMINED.

THAT'S ALRIGHT, BOYS.. THE VILLAGE IS OURS — THEY WON'T GET FAR ON FOOT!

LOOK AT THESE, COLONEL — BETTER THAN WE GOT!

STACK EVERYTHING AND SET THE TORCH TO IT!

OSAGE MISSION FLOUR

INSTEAD OF FACING THE COMING WINTER WELL-FED, SNUG AND SECURE IN THEIR LODGES, THE INDIANS ARE MADE DESTITUTE BY MACKENZIE'S SCORCHED-EARTH POLICY AS TONS OF CLOTHING, FOOD, SUPPLIES AND FORAGE ARE CONSIGNED TO THE FLAMES.

SERGEANT, PROCEED WITH THE DESTRUCTION OF THE CAMPS DOWNSTREAM. WE'VE GOT TO GET THEIR HORSES OUT OF HERE BEFORE DARK, OR QUANAH WILL HAVE THEM BACK!

MILES AWAY ON THE PRAIRIE, QUANAH SEES THE BLACK SMOKE RISE HIGH FROM PALO DURO AND KNOWS ITS MEANING.

A LEISURE PURSUIT REVEALS THE FULL EXTENT OF THE VICTORY.

WE ARE DOOMED..

WHEN THEY THROW COOKING UTENSILS AWAY, YOU KNOW THEY'RE BAD OFF..

MACKENZIE, TAKING NO CHANCES THIS TIME ON QUANAH GETTING BACK THE CAPTURED HORSES, ORDERS THEM **SHOT** — FIFTEEN-HUNDRED IN ALL, EXCEPT A FEW CHOICE ONES HELD BACK AS REWARDS FOR HIS SCOUTS.

GOD, I HATE THIS!

DAMN WASTE OF GOOD HORSEFLESH..

WHY DO I ALWAYS GET STUCK WITH THE LOUSY DETAILS?

WHEN THE SOLDIERS WITHDRAW, QUANAH VIEWS THE ACRES OF SLAUGHTERED ANIMALS WITH HORROR AND DESPAIR.

WHAT MANNER OF DEMON IS THIS WHITE CHIEF, TO SO WANTONLY DESTROY THE SACRED GOD-DOG!? HOW CAN ONE HONORABLY FIGHT SUCH A MAN??!

HE KNOWS, PERHAPS, THAT A COMANCHE AFOOT, IS NO LONGER A COMANCHE..

IT IS FINISHED... THE BUFFALO, OUR HORSES, LODGES, WEAPONS, ROBES.. EVEN OUR WINTER FOOD — EVERYTHING GONE! HOW CAN WE LIVE?

WE MUST GO TO THE AGENCY AND BEG FROM THE WHITEMAN, LIKE OUR KINSMEN DO.

TO LIVE IN A CAGE OF OUR OWN MAKING, LIKE THE WHITES?! NEVER!! I WILL DIE FIRST, HERE ON THE PLAINS — FREE!

BUT PROUD WORDS CANNOT FILL THE EMPTY BELLIES OF WOMEN AND CHILDREN. THE FOLLOWING SUMMER QUANAH LEADS THE TATTERED REMNANTS OF HIS PEOPLE TO FT. SILL AND THE MERCY OF THE CONQUERING WHITEMAN.

AS THE QUOHADA WARRIORS FILE QUIETLY BY AND THROW DOWN THEIR WEAPONS, QUANAH AT LAST COMES FACE TO FACE WITH THE MAN WHO HAS RELENTLESSLY CHASED HIM ON THE PLAINS FOR FOUR YEARS. NO WORDS ARE SPOKEN...

THAT'S HIM THERE, COLONEL.

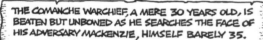

THE COMANCHE WARCHIEF, A MERE 30 YEARS OLD, IS BEATEN BUT UNBOWED AS HE SEARCHES THE FACE OF HIS ADVERSARY MACKENZIE, HIMSELF BARELY 35.

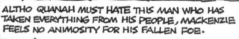

ALTHO QUANAH MUST HATE THIS MAN WHO HAS TAKEN EVERYTHING FROM HIS PEOPLE, MACKENZIE FEELS NO ANIMOSITY FOR HIS FALLEN FOE.

TAKE SOME TEAMS AND GATHER UP THE WEAK ONES. THEY'VE HAD A ROUGH TIME OF IT.

PENNED UP..

BUT NOT EVEN THE RESPECT AND GOODWILL OF YOUNG MACKENZIE CAN ALTER THE FATE THE VANQUISHED INDIANS MUST SUFFER. THEY ARE STRIPPED OF ALL THEIR POSSESSIONS AND PUT IN SQUALID CAMPS, UNDER HEAVY GUARD. SCURVY AND DYSENTERY RAVAGE THEIR SULLEN RANKS. THEY EAT IN HASTE AND SLEEP IN FEAR, UNSURE OF TOMORROW.

EVER WONDER WHAT IT'S LIKE, BEIN' INJUN?

NOPE.. BEIN' BLACK GIVE ME PLENTY TO KEEP MY MIND BUSY.

SOME, LIKE THE LEADERS WHO SIGNED TREATIES AND THEN BOLTED THE RESERVATION, ARE LOCKED IN AN UNFINISHED ICEHOUSE AND FED LIKE WILD ANIMALS.

HOPE THEY LIKE IT RARE.. HAW HAW

LOOK AT 'UM.. AIN'T THAT TH' MOST DISGUSTING THING YOU EVER SAW?

LATER THE CHIEF TROUBLEMAKERS ARE SENT IN CHAINS TO THE UNHEALTHY CLIMATE OF FLORIDA PRISONS.

YOU THINK YOU GOT IT MADE, KICKING BIRD, A BIG MAN WITH THE WHITES!! BUT YOU WON'T LIVE LONG, I'LL SEE TO THAT!

U.S.

QUANAH, LIKE HIS WARRIORS, HAS NOTHING TO DO BUT SIT AND STARE, DREAMING OF THE DAYS WHEN REDMEN RULED.

THE QUOHADAS ARE NOT SINGLED OUT FOR HARSH TREATMENT. MANY OFFICERS SPEAK OUT ON QUANAH'S BEHALF.

HE MADE NO PROMISES, SIGNED NO TREATIES — THEREFORE, HE HAS BROKEN NONE. SURE, HE KILLED — BUT IN DEFENSE OF HIS OWN TERRITORY, AS A SOLDIER OF HIS PEOPLE — AND A VERY WORTHY ONE I MIGHT ADD..

EVEN THE 'HATED TEXANS' TAKE A CERTAIN PRIDE IN HIM, NOW THAT HE IS NO LONGER A THORN IN THEIR SIDE.

QUANAH ?? WAHL HIS MA WUZ A PARKER, YOU KNOW. THERE'S BLUE BLOOD IN THET BOY'S VEINS. YESSIR, BLOOD WILL ALWAYS TELL, YOU CAN COUNT ON IT!!

YOU TALK ABOUT A FIGHTER, LET ME TELL YOU A' BOUT TH' TIME...

MACKENZIE, THINKING THE NOMADS MIGHT MAKE GOOD HERDSMEN, SELLS THEIR HORSES AND BRINGS IN A FLOCK OF PURE-BRED SHEEP FROM NEW MEXICO.

SHEEP ??

THE PROJECT FAILS MISERABLY...

MUTTON STEW GAGG!

WISH THEY'D BROUGHT US DOGS INSTEAD OF SHEEP!

THE CHIEFS THAT CO-OPERATED WITH THE AGENTS IN THE FINAL DAYS ARE REWARDED WITH HOUSES.

WHY DON'T YOU LIVE IN YOUR NICE NEW HOUSE, HORSEBACK ?

HEAP SNAKES IN THERE !!

QUANAH, BECAUSE HE HAD REFUSED TO COME IN TO THE RESERVATION UNTIL FORCED, IS NOT AWARDED A HOUSE.

YOU WANT MINE? I DON'T WANNA' GET SNAKEBIT!!

BEEF ISSUE DAY IS ABOUT THE ONLY TIME THAT THE WARRIORS CAN BREAK THE PARALYZING MONOTONY.

HE SAY HE WANT THAT ONE THERE..

FOR A BRIEF MOMENT THE THRILL OF THE CHASE RETURNS.

WOHAW! *

WOHAW WOHAW!!

THE WOMENFOLK SKIN AND CLEAN THE BONY LONG-HORNS, JUST AS THEY ONCE DID THE FAT BUFFALO.

GRADUALLY, QUANAH BREAKS OUT OF HIS APATHY.

IF MY MOTHER COULD LEARN THE WAYS OF THE INDIAN, I CAN LEARN THE WAYS OF THE WHITES.

* INDIAN WORD FOR CATTLE, FROM HEARING DROVERS HOLLER "WHOA-HAW" AT STEERS

104

HE DETERMINES TO CONTACT SOME OF HIS WHITE KINSMEN SO THAT HE MAY LEARN MORE OF THEIR MYSTERIOUS WAYS. ARMED WITH A PASS FROM THE AGENT, HE MAKES HIS WAY THROUGH TEXAS TO SEE HIS MOTHER'S BROTHER, JOHN PARKER. HE IS CAREFUL TO AVOID THE MANY NEW CABINS THAT HAVE SPRUNG UP ALONG THE OLD WAR TRAIL TO MEXICO.

AFTER JOHN PARKER RETURNED TO THE COMANCHES, HE HAD BEEN STRICKEN WITH SMALLPOX AND LEFT TO DIE BY THE INDIANS. HOWEVER, HE WAS NURSED BACK TO HEALTH BY A MEXICAN CAPTIVE, MARRIED HER, AND WENT TO LIVE A-MONG HER PEOPLE IN NORTHERN MEXICO. HIS LIFE HAS MADE HIM A CURIOUS MIXTURE OF ANGLO-COMANCHE-MEXICAN.

NOW A WELL-TO-DO STOCKMAN, JOHN PARKER TAKES HIS NEPHEW HUNTING, COMANCHE FASHION.

105

DURING THE VISIT, QUANAH IS GORED IN THE ABDOMEN BY A WILD SPANISH BULL, A CREATURE CONSIDERABLY DIFFERENT FROM THE DOCILE CRITTERS HE IS ACCUSTOMED TO AT BEEF ISSUES.

PAUBLO! GO GET THE MEDICINE MAN! PRONTO! PRONTO!!

HIS UNCLE'S BRUJO TREATS HIM WITH "WOQUI", A CONCOCTION MADE FROM THE JUICE OF THE PEYOTE CACTUS.

DRINK THIS, SON. TASTES REAL BAD, BUT IT'LL FIX YOU UP GOOD!

THUS IS QUANAH INTRODUCED TO THE DREAM-LIKE, PSYCHIC PROPERTIES OF PEYOTE, AN EXPERIENCE HE WILL LATER HELP SPREAD AMONG HIS TRIBE BACK ON THE RESERVATION.

HIS WOUND HEALED, VERSED ON CATTLE RAISING, AND SHOWERED WITH MANY GIFTS — INCLUDING A SACK OF THE WONDROUS PEYOTE BUTTONS — QUANAH SAYS GOODBYE TO JOHN PARKER, WHO HAS NEVER FORGOTTEN HIS EARLY DAYS AS A COMANCHE RAIDER.

THANKS FOR EVERYTHING, UNCLE JOHN.. NOW I THINK I'LL GO LOOK UP THE REST OF MOTHER'S FOLKS.

DON'T EXPECT TOO MUCH OF THEM, QUANAH. THEY'RE WHITE — NOT INDIAN, LIKE US!

USING A MAP DRAWN BY A HELPFUL STRANGER, QUANAH MAKES HIS WAY TO VAN ZANDT COUNTY AND THE HOME OF SILAS PARKER WHO HAD ESCAPED CAPTURE DURING THE FT. PARKER RAID.

YOU..MAYBE MY MOTHER'S PEOPLE? ME, QUANAH PARKER.

LAND'S SAKES! MY DEAR, DEPARTED SISTER'S BOY! LIGHT, AND COME IN THE HOUSE, SON..

QUANAH SLEEPS IN HIS MOTHER'S OLD BED.

NADUAH, HOW STRANGE TO THINK OF YOU IN THIS.. LITTLE CAGE...

ALREADY A LEGEND IN THIS PART OF TEXAS, QUANAH ASKS SILAS FOR GUIDANCE.

UNCLE, TEACH ME ABOUT "CIVILIZATION", SO THAT I MAY TELL MY PEOPLE..

FIRST THING OFF, YOU NEED TO KNOW ABOUT "MONEY"!

SEVERAL WEEKS LATER, HE RETURNS TO THE RESERVATION, ALMOST CONVINCED THE WHITEMAN'S WAY IS BEST.

THEY LIKE ME DOWN THERE. I CHURN BUTTER, LEARN ABOUT COWS, COTTON, & BLACK-EYED PEAS.

IF THEY LIKE YOU SO MUCH, WHY DIDN'T YOU STAY?

DOWN THERE, I JUST A PLAIN INJUN. HERE, I AM BIG CHIEF!

HAHA

BUT HE WANTS TO BE SURE. THE AGENT CONSENTS TO LET HIS CHARGES GO ON A FALL HUNT TO SUPPLEMENT THEIR MEAGER BEEF RATIONS. QUANAH LEADS THE GLEEFUL WARRIORS OFF TOWARD THEIR BELOVED BISON RANGE.

THE OLD MEN TELL THE YOUNG HOW IT WILL BE. THEY SIGH FOR THE TASTE OF MARROW BONES, FOR STEAMING LIVER, SPLASHED WITH GALL...

BELIEVE ME, THERE'S NOTHING LIKE IT!

BUT THE PLAINS ARE A GRAVEYARD OF BONES. SKIN HUNTERS HAVE DONE THEIR GRISLY WORK WELL. THE HERDS ARE GONE — NOT ONE BUFFALO IS FOUND!!

THE WARRIORS STARE DUMBLY INTO THEIR CAMPFIRES AS THE SHAMANS VAINLY SUMMON THE BUFFALO SPIRIT.

IN PALO DURO CANYON, JUST A FEW YEARS AGO THE LAST COMANCHE STRONGHOLD, QUANAH'S DISILLUSIONED BRAVES — NEAR STARVATION AND SUFFERING FROM THE COLD — MEET CHARLES GOODNIGHT, PIONEERING FOUNDER OF THE AREA'S FIRST BIG RANCH.

THERE AIN'T NO MORE BUFFALO, QUANAH — JUST MY COWS! AND IF YOU'LL KEEP YOUR MEN FROM KILLING THEM, I'LL SEE THAT YOU DON'T GO HUNGRY..

AS QUANAH LEADS HIS EMPTY-HANDED BAND BACK TO THE RESERVATION, HE KNOWS THE PAST IS GONE FOREVER. THERE IS NO TURNING BACK.

THERE IS NO PATH LEFT FOR US, EXCEPT THE WHITEMAN'S ROAD...

WHITEMAN'S ROAD

QUANAH STARTS TO TAKE AN ACTIVE ROLE IN TRIBAL AFFAIRS. ALTHO HIS WHITE BLOOD KEEPS HIM FROM BEING RECOGNIZED BY SOME STRICT TRADITIONALISTS AS HEADCHIEF, MANY INDIANS LOOK TO HIM FOR LEADERSHIP *BECAUSE* OF THIS BLOOD-LINK TO THE WHITES, HOPING IT MIGHT WORK TO QUANAH'S ADVANTAGE.

PUT ON YOUR BEST BUCKSKINS AND ROBES. WE MUST SPEAK TO THE SOLDIER CHIEF.

AFTER MOW-WAY STEPS DOWN AS HEADCHIEF, QUANAH'S INFLUENCE GROWS. THE COMANCHES FOLLOW HIM BECAUSE HE IS A PROVEN LEADER AMONG THEM — AND A MAN THE WHITES SEEM TO RESPECT AND LISTEN TO.

IT IS NOT FITTING THAT YOUNG BRAVES SHOULD ARREST TRIED AND PROVEN WARRIORS! IF THEY MUST FACE JUSTICE, THEN I, THEIR CHIEF, SHOULD BRING THEM IN!

???..

AND IN CURBING INFRINGEMENTS ON THE RESERVATION BY WHITE CATTLE DROVERS.

THIS IS COMANCHE LAND. YOU CANNOT DRIVE YOUR CATTLE THROUGH HERE!

I GOTTA GET THESE STEERS TO KANSAS, CHIEF. NAME YOUR PRICE.

QUANAH LEVIES A TOLL OF $1.00 PER HEAD ON THE VAST HERDS DRIVEN NORTH ACROSS THE INDIANS' RICH GRASSLANDS.

EVENTUALLY THE TEXAS CATTLEMEN FIND IT TO THEIR ADVANTAGE TO LEASE THE LAND FROM THE INDIANS.

WE'LL PAY $100,000 A YEAR FOR GRAZING RIGHTS.

OKAY, BUT NO CHECKS..

QUANAH GOES TO WASHINGTON, THE FIRST OF MANY TRIPS, TO SECURE PERMISSION FOR THE LEASES.

THIS IS A VERY STICKY ISSUE.. YOU'RE HEADMAN NOW QUANAH, SO UNTIL SOMEBODY MAKES UP HIS MIND, DO WHAT YOU THINK BEST.

AND SO, QUANAH MAKES HIMSELF SOME *POWERFUL FRIENDS* IN HIS DEALINGS WITH RICH CATTLE BARONS LIKE DAN WAGGONER, CHARLES GOODNIGHT, AND S.B. "BURK" BURNETT.

THIS IS HELPING BOTH OF US, QUANAH. IF THERE'S EVER ANYTHING WE CAN DO FOR YOU, JUST LET US KNOW...

QUANAH IS MADE CHIEF JUDGE OF A THREE-MAN COURT OF INDIAN OFFENSES. HIS VERDICTS ARE UNORTHODOX.

YOU, DRUNK AND OBNOXIOUS— TEN DAYS IN JAIL. YOU, KILL WORTHLESS HORSE THIEF— *FOUR DAYS!*

SKEPTICAL OF THE GHOST DANCE RELIGION, THEN IN VOGUE AMONG NORTHERN PLAINS TRIBES, HE COUNSELS HIS PEOPLE TO STAY CLEAR OF ITS DOCTRINES.

REMEMBER WHAT HAPPENED TO US AT ADOBE WALLS, WHEN WE LISTENED TO A "PROPHET"...

QUANAH IS CONTENT WITH HIS "PEYOTE RELIGION" AND DEFENDS IT TO WHITE, MEN-OF-THE-CLOTH AS WELL.

WHEN YOU GO TO CHURCH, YOU TALK *ABOUT* GOD. WHEN I GO TO MY CHURCH, I TALK *WITH* GOD! BESIDES, IT'S GOOD FOR STOMACH-ACHES.

VARIOUS MISSIONARIES TRY TO WIN QUANAH OVER TO *CHRISTIANITY*, WHICH HE LEARNS WOULD REQUIRE HIM TO GIVE UP ALL HIS WIVES BUT ONE.

IN THAT CASE, I KEEP MY *RELIGION!*

111

QUANAH REMAINS A STEADFAST ADVOCATE OF COMANCHE RITUAL BELIEFS, HEIGHTENED BY THE PSYCHIC REVELATIONS OF THE PEYOTE CACTUS.

HIS UNCEASING EFFORTS TO IMPROVE THE LOT OF HIS PEOPLE COMMANDS THE RESPECT OF THE WHITE COMMUNITY. A NEW TOWN IN TEXAS IS NAMED AFTER HIM.

MAY THE GREAT SPIRIT ALWAYS SMILE ON YOUR TOWN. MAY PEACE AND CONTENTMENT DWELL WITH YOU AND YOUR CHILDREN FOREVER! ME, QUANAH, SAY THANK YOU.

IN 1886 BURK BURNETT AND OTHER CATTLEMEN INVITE QUANAH TO ATTEND THE FAT STOCK SHOW IN FT. WORTH. HE AND YELLOW BEAR, GODFATHER TO WEAKEAH, ARE GIVEN LUXURY ACCOMMODATIONS AT THE PICKWICK HOTEL.

PURTY FANGY HUH CHIEF?

I SEEN BETTER.

THEY ARE WINED AND DINED IN STYLE. STEAKS, DONE RARE, ARE THE INEVITABLE CHOICE OF THE MEAT-STARVED INDIANS ON ALL SUCH GALA OCCASIONS.

WOHAW!

WHAT'LL YOU BE HAVING, CHIEF?

BEFORE RETIRING, YELLOW BEAR — UNACCUSTOMED TO MODERN GADGETRY — BLOWS OUT THE GAS LAMP.

PPSSSSSSSSHHH

I SLEEP ON FLOOR.. BURRP..DAMN BED HURT MY BACK!

THE NEXT MORNING QUANAH AND YELLOW BEAR FAIL TO SHOW UP FOR BREAKFAST...

GUESS WE BET-TER GO SEE WHAT'S KEEPIN' THEM...

OPENING THE DOOR, THE COWMEN ARE ALMOST OVERWHELMED BY THE DEADLY GAS FUMES.

OPEN THAT WINDOW— QUICK!

QUANAH FINALLY COMES AROUND...

HE'S DEAD'RN HELL, QUANAH.

BUCK, WHERE.. IS..YELLOW BEAR?

SADDENED BY THE LOSS OF HIS FIRST WIFE'S RELATIVE, HE ESCORTS YELLOW BEAR'S BODY BACK HOME.

LUCKY FOR US THEY DIDN'T BOTH DIE. WE'D HAD A DEVIL OF A TIME, EXPLAIN-ING IT TO THE TRIBE!

TIVOLI

GUN STORE

WHILE IN FT. WORTH, QUANAH ADVERTISES IN THE NEWSPAPER FOR A PICTURE OF HIS MOTHER. SUL ROSS, WHO LED THE RANGERS AT THE TIME OF CYNTHIA ANN'S CAPTURE, SECURES A COPY OF THE DAGUERREOTYPE MADE OF HER IN FT. WORTH AND SENDS IT TO AN INCREDULOUS QUANAH.

HOW CAN THIS BE? NADUAH AND MY BABY SISTER, BY THE MAGIC THAT HOLDS THE SPIRIT TO A CARD!

QUANAH IS FASCINATED BY THIS AND OTHER ASPECTS OF THE MYSTERIOUS WHITEMAN'S ROAD.

ICE.. IN THE HOT MONTHS OF SUMMER..

BURNETT OFFERS TO BUILD QUANAH A HOUSE.

YOU'RE HEADMAN NOW QUANAH— BESIDES, YOU NEED IT, WHAT WITH ALL THOSE WIVES AND KIDS YOU GOT...

QUANAH PICKS A FAVORITE CAMPING SPOT, AT THE FOOT OF THE BEAUTIFUL WICHITA MOUNTAINS. THE LUMBER IS BROUGHT FROM EAST TEXAS BY RAIL AND HAULED TO THE SITE BY WAGON FROM VERNON, BELOW DOAN'S CROSSING.

THE 22 ROOM SHOWPLACE BECOMES KNOWN AS THE "COMANCHE WHITEHOUSE".

I KEEP A TEEPEE OUT BACK IN CASE I GET LONESOME..

THE WAGGONER BROTHERS GIVE QUANAH A THOUSAND DOLLAR STAGECOACH SO HE CAN RIDE TO TOWN IN STYLE.

WE GOTTA FILL IN THESE CHUGHOLES ONE OF THESE DAYS, HUSBAND...

RATTLE BUMP

QUANAH FIGHTS THE LAND-HUNGRY BOOMERS WHO ARE EXERTING PRESSURE ON THE GOVERNMENT TO DISMANTLE INDIAN TERRITORY AND OPEN IT TO WHITE SETTLERS.

IF THEY CUT UP THE LAND, MR. BURK, IT'S OVER FOR ALL OF US...

GO UP THERE AND TALK TO THEM QUANAH. WE'LL THROW ALL OUR WEIGHT BEHIND YOU.

SUPPORTED BY THE CATTLERAISERS' LOBBY AND THEIR ATTORNEYS, HE STALLS DISMEMBERMENT OF THE RESERVATION.

THIS TREATY SAY "PERMANENT HOME." PERMANENT NOT LONG ENOUGH. MY PEOPLE NEED MORE TIME TO LEARN THE WHITEMANS ROAD.

BUT AGENTS SUCCEED IN GETTING THE SIGNATURES OF SOME MINOR CHIEFTAINS ON AN AGREEMENT TO SELL THE LAND. QUANAH AGAIN GOES TO WASHINGTON TO FIGHT THE MEASURE.

THAT DAMN JEROME TRICK THOSE POOR, DUMB INDIANS! HE NOT SPEAK FOR COMANCHES— I, QUANAH, SPEAK!

DESPITE ALL HIS OPPOSITION, THE TERRITORY IS EVENTUALLY SPLIT UP, EACH INDIAN—YOUNG AND OLD—RECEIVING AN ACREAGE ALLOTMENT. THERE IS MUCH LENDING OF CHILDREN.

FAT DOG GET ME ANOTHER 160 ACRES!

QUANAH URGES RESISTANCE TO THE FORMATION OF AN INDIAN CAVALRY BATTALION.

YOUR MISSIONARIES TEACH OUR BRAVES IT IS WRONG TO GO TO WAR. IF THIS IS TRUE, WHY SHOULD WE FIGHT FOR THE WHITEMAN??

WE QUIT FIGHTING LONG AGO!

A STRONG BELIEVER IN EDUCATION SINCE HIS VISIT WITH HIS MOTHER'S PEOPLE, QUANAH IS CHOSEN PRESIDENT OF THE LOCAL SCHOOL DISTRICT.

I GOT THREE OF MY KIDS BACK EAST AT CARLISLE SCHOOL SO THEY GET SMART, LIKE WHITEFOLKS!

HAHA

RED STOR

HE IS ELECTED DEPUTY SHERIFF OF LAWTON, OKLAHOMA.

WHO KNOWS? ONE OF THESE DAYS, MAYBE I BE A TEXAS RANGER!!

QUANAH, TRUE TO THE RESTLESSNESS OF HIS QUOHADA BLOOD, IS A CEASELESS TRAVELER. HE TAKES HIS BRAVES TO EVERY PUBLIC EVENT THAT INVITES HIM — 4TH OF JULY CELEBRATIONS, OLD SETTLERS REUNIONS, PICNICS, RODEOS, CONFEDERATE VETERANS GATHERINGS, STATE FAIRS, WORLD FAIRS — ANY EXCUSE TO MOVE AROUND.

YOUR BOYS PUT ON A EXCITIN' SHOW, CHIEF! MADE FOLKS' BLOOD RUN COLD— JUST LIKE IN THE OLD DAYS!

..WE'RE A LITTLE OUT OF PRACTICE..

OLD SETTLERS SEYMOUR T

HE OFTEN USES THESE EVENTS TO SPREAD HIS POLITICAL VIEWS.

WE LOVE THE WHITEMAN BUT WE FEAR YOUR SUCCESS. ONCE THIS PRETTY COUNTRY YOU TOOK AWAY FROM US, BUT SEE HOW DRY IT IS NOW. ONLY FIT FOR RED ANTS, CATTLE-MEN AND COYOTES!!

AT THE ROUGH RIDERS REUNION IN OKLAHOMA CITY, HE MEETS FUTURE PRESIDENT THEODORE ROOSEVELT FOR THE FIRST TIME.

WISH YOUR RIDERS HAD BEEN WITH ME AT SAN JUAN HILL, QUANAH. WE'D HAVE SCARED HELL OUT OF 'UM!

QUANAH RETURNS THE PRESIDENT'S OBVIOUS RESPECT.

HIM, INJUNS' PRESIDENT— THE GREATEST MAN IN WORLD! I, CHIEF OF COMANCHES, BUT HE THE BIG *CHIEF* OF ALL OF US!

TEDDY ESCAPES THE WEIGHT OF HIS OFFICE TO GO WOLF HUNTING WITH QUANAH IN THE BIG PASTURE.

TIME AND SPACE ARE CLOSING IN ON OUR KIND, QUANAH. PRETTY SOON, ALL THIS WILL BE JUST MEMORIES.. LITTLE MEN, SHOPKEEPERS WILL BE RUNNING THE SHOW.

MAYBE SO, MAYBE, NO. BUT I GOT ME A SON-IN-LAW SHOP KEEPER, JUST IN CASE!!

HOME, HOME, ON 'N' RANGE

DESPITE QUANAH'S RESPECT FOR ROOSEVELT THE MAN, HIS POLITICS REMAIN DEMOCRATIC.

I TELL YOU ONE MATTER, LADIES AND GENTLEMEN· YOU SEE MY TWO HANDS? THE REPUBLICAN HAND FOR RICH MAN — SQUEEZES MONEY TIGHT! DEMOCRAT HAND FOR POOR MAN — WANTS TO TURN IT LOOSE!!

TEXAS ST FAIR

HE BECOMES A MAJOR STOCKHOLDER IN THE NEW QUANAH, ACME & PACIFIC RAILWAY. HE LIKES TO PET THE "IRON HORSE", TREATING IT LIKE A WAR STALLION OF OLD.

NICE TRAIN.. NICE ENGINE..

QUANAH TURNS DOWN LUCRATIVE OFFERS TO TOUR EUROPE WITH A WILD WEST SHOW.

STATEHOOD AND PROHIBITION COME TO OKLAHOMA IN 1907, AND WITH IT, CONCERN OVER THE WIDESPREAD USE OF PEYOTE BY THE INDIANS. QUANAH WORKS TO HAVE IT RECOGNIZED AS A SACRAMENT OF THEIR RELIGION, BUT IT IS NOT UNTIL 3 YEARS LATER THAT A CHARTER IS SECURED TO PUT THE PEYOTE CULT AND THE NATIVE AMERICAN CHURCH ON A LEVEL WITH OTHER RELIGIONS.

..BUT CHIEF, WITH YOU AND YOUR FAMILY ON THE BILL, WE'D PACK 'UM IN LIKE SARDINES! HOW DOES $5,000 SOUND?

SORRY.. I'M NO MONKEY.

WAHL, MARCUS, NOW THAT IT'S LEGAL.. I DON'T RECKON QUANAH'LL HAVE TO BAIL YOU OUTTA' HERE ANYMORE.. HAW HAW

WASHINGTON OFFICIALS TRY TO GET QUANAH TO SET AN EXAMPLE BY PUTTING ASIDE ALL OF HIS WIVES EXCEPT ONE. THE TOUCHY SUBJECT IS EVENTUALLY DROPPED.

YOU CAN ONLY KEEP ONE, QUANAH. YOU MUST TELL THE OTHERS TO GO

NOT ME — YOU TELL 'UM!

AHEM..UHM.. SPUTTER

HE REMAINS THE PATRIARCH OF A NUMEROUS CLAN — EIGHTEEN CHILDREN IN ALL, AND A HOST OF GRANDCHILDREN. SEVERAL DAUGHTERS MARRY PROMINENT MEN IN THE WHITE COMMUNITY. ONE OF HIS SONS BECOMES A METHODIST MINISTER.

BET HIS FOOD BILL WOULD CHOKE A HORSE!

QUANAH'S OLD FRIEND CHARLES GOODNIGHT OCCASIONALLY STAGES MINI-HUNTS FOR THE COMANCHES FROM HIS CAREFULLY-PRESERVED SMALL HERD OF BISON. BUT WHILE GAZING AT THE BEAUTY OF A PALO DURO SUNSET, SADNESS CREEPS IN AS THESE TWO GREAT MEN REMEMBER WHAT WAS — AND WHAT MIGHT HAVE BEEN...

IN HIS LATER YEARS, QUANAH'S THOUGHTS TURN TO DEATH. HE AND SEVERAL OF HIS OLD WARRIORS TAKE OFF IN SEARCH OF CEDAR LAKE. SOME COWBOYS FIND THEM STUCK IN THE SAND NEAR LUBBOCK.

WHERE YOU FELLERS GOIN' CHIEF?

IT IS THE CUSTOM OF MY PEOPLE TO RETURN TO THE PLACE OF THEIR BIRTH AND SLEEP THREE NIGHTS BEFORE THEIR LIFE IS FINISHED...

QUANAH TRIES TO HAVE HIS MOTHER'S BONES REMOVED FROM TEXAS BUT RUNS INTO TROUBLE. AN ELOQUENT LETTER, READ IN THE CHURCHES OF EAST TEXAS, DOES MUCH TO QUIET LOCAL OPPOSITION TO HIS REQUEST.

"MY MOTHER. SHE FED ME, CARRY ME IN HER ARMS, PAT ME TO SLEEP. I PLAY, SHE HAPPY— I CRY, SHE SAD. SHE LOVE HER BOY. THEY TOOK MY MOTHER AWAY, TOOK TEXAS AWAY. NOT LET HER BOY SEE HER, NOW SHE DEAD... HER BOY WANT TO BURY HER, SIT BY HER MOUND. MY PEOPLE, HER PEOPLE—WE NOW ALL ONE PEOPLE. BOY LONESOME, LOVE MOTHER. SHE MINE, I BURY HER... I PLEAD.."

SNIFF SNIFF

FINALLY HE SUCCEEDS, AND CYNTHIA ANN'S REMAINS ARE REBURIED NEAR HIS HOME AT CACHE, SO THAT HE MAY REST BESIDE HER WHEN HIS OWN TIME COMES.

SHE LOVE INDIANS AND WILD LIFE SO WELL, SHE NO WANT TO GO BACK TO WHITE FOLKS. ALL SAME PEOPLE ANYWAY, GOD SAY. GLAD TO SEE EVERYBODY HERE AT THIS FINE FUNERAL. THAT'S ALL.

QUANAH, NOW 65 YEARS OLD, SOON FLIES ON THE WINGS OF THE EAGLE TO MEET HIS ANCESTORS. HE REMAINS AN INDIAN TO THE END...

NIA KESA, HI-PE MI-ON. KOMUP NIA UN MANAKWI, MI'ON...

GREAT SPIRIT IN HEAVEN... THIS, OUR BROTHER IS COMING.

HE IS BURIED IN ALL THE POMP AND SPLENDOR OF HIS SAVAGE BIRTH. PEOPLE GATHER FROM FAR AND NEAR TO PAY THEIR LAST RESPECTS TO QUANAH — POLITICIANS, INDIAN LEADERS, RANCHERS, FINANCIERS, AND JUST PLAIN FOLKS. HIS FUNERAL PROCESSION STRETCHES OUT OVER TWO MILES LONG AS IT WENDS ITS WAY UP TO THE POST OAK CEMETERY.

SO ENDS THE SAGA OF THE *LAST CHIEF OF THE COMANCHES*, WHO PERHAPS DID MORE TO RECONCILE THE RED AND WHITE RACES THAN ANY OTHER MAN. BUT HIS SPIRIT LIVES ON! EACH YEAR THE DESCENDANTS OF QUANAH AND THEIR PARKER RELATIVES GATHER TO HONOR THE MEMORY OF CYNTHIA ANN AND HER REMARKABLE SON.

Credits and References

This book started out as a three months project, but has taken over three years to finish. Seems like the more I learned about the Comanches and their last chief, Quanah Parker, the more I realized that it would take considerable time and energy to do their story the justice it deserves.

Still, there is nothing new in this book. Many other writers, to whom I am deeply indebted, have told the story. I have only sifted their work, placing emphasis on events according to my limited grasp of the rapidly shifting historical panorama. What good my effort possesses should be credited to them, but its faults are mine alone.

Also, I must acknowledge the rich heritage of Western art from which I have freely drawn, and extend my apologies to the "Old Masters" for my shameless fleecing of their work. Particularly victimized were Charles Russell, Frederic Remington, Harold von Schmidt, Nick Eggenhofer, and John Clymer. Thomas Mails should also be mentioned for his comprehensive reference book on the plains cultures.

Special thanks go to Chester Kielman and the Barker Texas History Center, Dorman Winfrey and the Texas State Library, Gillett Griswold of the Fort Sill Museum, and Sam Nesmith of the Institute of Texan Cultures. Also to W. W. Newcomb, Jr., T. R. Fehrenbach, and Mildred Mayhall—authors of excellent books on Texas Indians—and to Baldwin Parker, Jr., whose songs melted the walls of his modern home and transported me back to prairies of the past, bathed by the light of a full Comanche Moon.

For the reader, who would like to know more about the historical period portrayed in *Comanche Moon*, the following list of source books is included:

Babb, T.A. – In The Bosom of the Comanches
Berlandier, Jean Louis – The Indians of Texas in 1830
Brill, Charles J. – Conquest of the Southern Plains
Brown, Dee – Bury My Heart at Wounded Knee
Capps, Benjamin – The Great Chiefs
Capps, Benjamin – The Indians
Capps, Benjamin – The Warren Wagontrain Raid
Deshields, James T. – Cynthia Ann Parker: The Story of Her Capture
Fehrenbach, T.R. – The Comanches: Destruction of a People
Gard, Wayne – The Great Buffalo Hunt
Haley, J. Evetts – Men of Fiber
Haley, James L. – The Buffalo War
Harston, J. Emmor – Comanche Land
Holt, Roy – Heap Many Chiefs
Hyde, George – Rangers and Regulars
Institute of Texan Cultures (ed.) – The Indian Texans

Jackson, Clyde L. and Grace – Quanah Parker: Last Chief of the Comanches
Jackson, Grace – Cynthia Ann Parker
Jones, Douglas C. – The Medicine Lodge Treaty
Keating, Bern – An Illustrated History of the Texas Rangers
Koury, Michael J. – Arms for Texas
Lafarge, Oliver – A Pictorial History of the American Indian
Leckie, William – The Buffalo Soldiers
Mails, Thomas E. – The Mystic Warriors of the Plains
Mayhall, Mildred P. – Indian Wars of Texas
Mueller, Oswald (trans,) – Roemer's Texas
Neighbors, Kenneth F. – Indian Exodus
Neighbors, Kenneth F. – Robert Neighbors and the Texas Frontier
Newcomb, W. W. Jr. – The Indians of Texas
Nye, W. S. – Carbine and Lance: The Story of Old Fort Sill
Nye, W. S. – Plains Indian Raiders
Parker, James W. (ed.) – Rachel Plummer Narrative
Richardson, R. N. – The Comanche Barrier to South Plains Settlement
Robertson, R. L. and Pauline – Panhandle Pilgrimage
Schmitt, Martin F. and Dee Brown – Fighting Indians of the West
Thrall, Homer S. – A Pictorial History of Texas
Tilghman, Zoe A. – Quanah, Eagle of the Comanches
Tiling, Moritz – History of the German Element In Texas
Utley, Robert – Frontiersmen in Blue, 1845–1865
Utley, Robert – Frontier Regulars, 1866–1890
Waldraven-Johnson, Margaret – The White Comanche
Wallace, Ernest – Ranald S. Mackenzie on the Texas Frontier
Wallace, Ernest and E. Adamson Hoebel – The Comanches, Lords of the Southern Plains
Webb, Walter Prescott – The Texas Rangers
Weems, John Edward – Death Song
Wellman, Paul – Death on the Prairie
Wilbarger, J. W. – Indian Depredations in Texas

(FSM)

CYNTHIA ANN PARKER

Cynthia Ann Parker sat for this rare portrait in Austin at the time of the secession convention, February 28, 1861, just two months after her recapture. Reuben J. Palmer was a legislator when she received a land grant from the state and his daughter, Mrs. Agnes Stroud, owned the original.

Daniel Parker, Uncle of Cynthia Ann

Isaac Parker, Uncle of Cynthia Ann

Another view of Daniel Parker, founder
of the Fundamentalist Baptist Church

Benjamin F. Parker, Daniel's son,
Cynthia Ann's first cousin

(SI)

(UTA)

(SI)

(SI)

Quanah and his "show wife," Tonarcy

(FSM)

(FSM)

(UTA)

(FSM)

The many sides of Quanah Parker

(UTA)

(FSM)

(FSM)

(SI)

Some of Quanah's children; Wanda, Weyote, Harold, Len and Baldwin